War Game

War Game, Volume 1

Renier Palland

Published by S & S Books, 2022.

WAR GAME

First edition. May 6, 2022.

Copyright © 2022 Renier Palland.

ISBN: 979-8201953263

Written by Renier Palland.

Table of Contents

PROLOGUE

The Murray building was a decrepit relic from the seventies. Ten apartments per floor, five floors up.

The disillusioned and bread-liners lived there. It kept them out of harm's way on the streets. Plus, the owner of the Murray building kept the rent low and the lights on.

At night, the building looked like a skeleton - each apartment's light appeared to be frozen in time, like jagged rows of yellowed teeth. And during the day, the Murray building resembled a slab of concrete vomited by a skyscraper; it wasn't a pleasant building to live in.

The superintendent, a Mr. Karpov, worked the hallways like a prison guard, threatening individuals who "stepped out of line"; each transgression changing with the seasons. One couldn't keep a light on past twelve, or one's doors had to be locked from 8pm onwards. Mr. Karpov always had an excuse.

If someone did step out of line, Karpov would charge them a "nominal fee" to assure their safety from the Russian mafia. There was no Russian mafia, Karpov used the money to fuel his drug trade in the basement.

"Two hits for a dollar!" He often shared his misbehaving secrets with some of the older residents, like Mrs. Rose, who scolded him on a daily basis.

Then there was Jessie. A black kid from a bad neighborhood. He was the Murray building's in-house doorman. Just shy of 19, Jessie welcomed the residents with a witty quip. "Mrs. Rose! Where dem bones you hid from us? Discovery Channel would do a number on your fossilized remains!" Everyone loved Jessie. They even cooked meals for him, especially Mrs. Rose, the only tenant left who'd moved in when the building was erected in the seventies.

Nina Corletti moved to the Murray building against the advice of her friends. She had a five-year-old daughter, Mia, and not a cent to spare. Her well-to-do Italian family cut her off when she turned 18. She arrived at home one morning with a baby bump the size of Mount Everest and found all of her belongings on the curb.

Nina's family viewed her teenage pregnancy as a disgrace and a Catholic sin. She spoke to her mom a couple of times afterwards, but she always ended up crying and yelling at her mother in Italian. Now she worked two jobs - as a waitress and a cleaner. Mia stayed with Mrs. Rose during the day. She baked cookies and gave her daughter lessons in etiquette - the perfect combo for a five-year-old kid.

Nina never listened to advice - she blamed her Italian personality - so when she saw the ad on Craigslist, she jumped at the chance to move into the Murray building. Thirty dollars per week! A fully renovated and fully furnished two-bedroom apartment on the fifth floor. How could she resist? After all, Vincent was growing tired of her and Mia bunking in his living room; he had no place to smoke his bong.

So, Nina thanked him and left his place the very same day.

Once, during summer, Nina's childhood friend came to visit her. Marita Merkovitz, a first generation Polish immigrant, gave the apartment one look and laughed until she cried. Nina wanted to know what was so funny, but Marita merely burst out laughing. Nina eventually found out that Marita's family had moved into the Murray building when they arrived in the States.

The drug lords had wanted money every week - this was in the late nineties. And Marita, at the tender age of two, watched her mother and father get gunned down by a certain drug lord who allegedly still roamed the streets.

Marita had a stress reaction, and consequently disappeared from Nina's life, blocked her on Facebook and moved on. Nina never got over Marita's hysterical outburst; it was strangely juxtaposed against the stark fluorescent lights in the apartment that evening, akin to seeing a contrast of an old photograph. In fact, Nina once told Mrs. Rose that Marita's outburst reminded her of the ingénues from the early 20's; scream and cry and faint. Mrs. Rose laughed at the metaphor and instructed Nina to "get new friends".

So she did.

A male friend. His name was Arthur, an elderly gentleman with thin, white hair and a Sam Elliot moustache. He helped Nina secure her current jobs, he helped her financially - no strings attached - and also left something for Mia in his will. He was merely a father figure to Nina. Nothing more, nothing less. He died on Christmas Eve, two years ago.

Nina remembered the call from his daughter. "You fucked my father for his money. Now he's dead. Get out of our fucking lives, you worthless little bitch!" Nina went to the funeral but stayed behind in the shadows.

Arthur was her lifeline, both as a friend and a financial aid. His loss was significant. She wept for days, even slept in Mrs. Rose's apartment for a couple of months. She couldn't face the world. But somehow, from some deep place within, Nina gained the strength she needed to fight the contested will in court. The judge ruled in her favor - Mia received $1 million tied up in a trust fund until her 18th birthday. Nina cried. Her daughter would never have to face the same hardships. She was set.

For life.

CHAPTER ONE
4:13PM

"Mommy! When can we go to the park?"

"Not today, hon. Mommy's got to work today. Why don't you go play with Mrs. Rose for a bit?" Nina tied up her sleek, black hair and doused her face in cold water. Her dark eyes and tanned complexion gave her an exotic aura that rubbed off on most men. She was also fit, muscular and could overpower someone twice her size.

Nina's brother taught her how to fight, so from a young age Nina hit the punching bag in the garage until her knuckles bled. She was thankful for her brother's training, it helped her out of crazy situations. And everyone who knew her could feel that power vibrating from behind her eyes; it was a palpable strength. Both physically and psychologically.

"Mommy?" Mia's little face appeared in the bathroom mirror. Nina had zoned out again, she did that sometimes. Mrs. Rose called it 'Eternal Fatigue'. Nina called it 'Thinking in Silence'.

"Yes, Mia?"

"Mommy, Mr. Karpov said that little girls get abducted by bad men when they roam the building. Is it true?"

"Mia. Listen to your mother." Nina swirled around and held her daughter's face in her hands. "Mr. Karpov likes to scare people. Vulnerable people especially."

"What's vulnerable?"

"It means people who aren't...uhm, all grown up yet? People who don't have enough strength to stand up to him."

Nina felt as if her blood was poured into a slow cooker. Karpov had another thing coming. She knew she had to face him, and no, she wasn't scared of an old drug addicted Russian.

"I'm going to kick Mr. Karpov's ass!" Nina smiled as she spoke the words.

"Mommy! 'Ass' is a bad word!"

"I know. I know. Sorry, honey, but sometimes you gotta call a spade a spade."

Nina picked her daughter up and planted her on the living room couch. The daylight filtered through the window and danced on the kitchen table like someone who had just downed a couple of MDMA tablets.

"Mommy?"

"Yes, Mia?"

"Mommy, will Mrs. Rose die like Uncle Arthur?"

Nina stopped in her tracks. She hadn't discussed death with Mia yet. She wanted to shield her from the nasty things in life like death and sex and drugs and teenage pregnancies and dead Polish families and Mr. Karpov and Creationism. She kneeled at her daughter's feet.

"Baby, Mrs. Rose is rather old. And when people grow old, they usually pass away, like Uncle Arthur. And then they go to heaven, where all of their friends and family members are waiting."

Mia started to cry.

"What if there's no heaven, Mommy? What if we die and there's nothing? Will you go to heaven when you die?"

Nina couldn't understand how her daughter had gone from *Dora the Explorer* to Nietzsche in such a short amount of time. A nihilistic little kid didn't gel with society very well, Nina knew this from experience.

"Baby, listen to me, okay? You don't have to worry about all that stuff now. You're five! You still have an entire life ahead of you. Think happy thoughts. Don't dwell on death so much, you hear?"

They hugged. Mia snuggled against her mother's breasts. Nina held her and whispered in her ear, "When I get back from work, I'm going to make us some pancakes."

Mia nodded. "I'd like that, Mommy."

CHAPTER TWO
4:30PM

Jessie Clarence always arrived on time for his shift as doorman at the Murray building. His grandfather, who passed away two years ago, instilled gentlemanly behavior in Jessie. He always said, "Be punctual, kid. They'll remember you." Jessie lived according to this motto; no matter what happened during the days, Jessie was always on time.

Mr. Karpov, who lived on a different timeline due to all the drugs he took, always scolded Jessie for being late. Jessie was used to it. He'd simply stare at the old man and mumble something under his breath. Usually a profanity. Luckily for him, Mr. Karpov was hard of hearing, so the old Russian never quite caught Jessie's profanities.

It was a topic of contention for Karpov, but Jessie didn't allow it to faze him. Karpov couldn't fire him – only the owner could – and no white or black member of society had ever met *him*; Jessie's girlfriend always joked that the owner of the Murray building was the building itself.

Jessie would reply with "You read too many horror novels," and scoff at the very idea that a building was alive. God, this wasn't a Stephen King novel - and no one had the Shine. Except for Mrs. Rose. She knew stuff about Jessie that couldn't have been possible. Either that or she worked for the NSA. And Jessie wouldn't put the latter idea past her.

Mr. Karpov waited in reception. Arms folded over his massive chest, he eyed Jessie silently as he made his way to the locker room.

"One of these days, you get fired! Late. Late. Late! Always!" The Russian's pupils were as black as that night when the power went off all across the Eastern Seaboard. Jessie shivered at the thought of masked madmen that could have hidden in the shadows.

"Good afternoon, Mr. Karpov. You're in a good mood today," Jessie smiled.

"Don't fuck me over! You come late."

"Mr. Karpov, if you had looked at your watch, you would have seen that I parked my bicycle at exactly half past four. On time in my book."

Karpov huffed and puffed like a nuclear bomb before it explodes.

"Don't get - what you Americans call it? - cheek with me!"

"Cheeky, Mr. Karpov. Now if you'd please step aside. I have work to do."

Jessie brushed past him and slipped into the locker room. It reeked of old shoes and meth. Jessie changed into his black and red uniform, spun the dial on his locker and went into the reception area. A large mahogany desk covered Jessie's workstation. Someone had carved "Fuck Jews" into the side, but no one ever saw it because Jessie pasted a "DO NOT ENTER" sign over the anti-Semitic utterance. Karpov loved to rip it off and laugh about Jewish people; Jessie found that intolerable.

He took a seat behind the computer and typed in his password – 'Lyla' – his girlfriend's name. The screen flicked on and off as the PC booted up. It was an old computer, upon which Jessie played Solitaire on quiet nights, and surfed Facebook if the Wi-Fi allowed it. As with everything in the Murray building, even the Wi-Fi had issues with staying sober.

Mr. Karpov disappeared into the basement. Jessie was relieved. He couldn't listen to the Russian's crap anymore.

The elevator, which only worked on weekends for some unknown reason, pinged as it arrived on the first floor. It was a Saturday, and Jessie knew Nina from apartment 47 was on her way to work. She sometimes left her daughter Mia with him when she popped out for shopping.

The doors slid open, and the beautiful Italian stepped out. Wearing high heels - Rudy's Diner forced their waitresses to wear high heels - Nina slipped out of the elevator like a skinned mermaid. She walked forcefully and with purpose. Jessie noticed that she had applied a dark rouge to her lips - not the usual light pink. Was Nina off to see a guy after work? Possibly.

Jessie smiled and waved. Nina returned the politeness and said, "Jessie! You look so refreshed. How the hell do you do it?"

"Aw shucks, Nina. I guess it's my girlfriend keeping me young."

"Dude! You're nineteen!" Nina laughed.

"Have you ever worked for a drug addicted Russian before? He believes he's protecting us from the goddamned Russian mafia!"

Nina snorted with laughter.

"Can't say I have. Well, I got to run. Work and all that. Keep an eye on Mia for me? If you see her, tell her that the pancake deal is off. She knows she's not allowed to go out after dark!"

"Will do so. And Nina?"

"Yeah?"

"You look beautiful."

Nina blushed. "Thank you, Jessie. Always the charmer. Ciao for now!"

Nina walked out the front door and disappeared into the blazing, electrifying sunset. Jessie had a tiny crush on her, but he'd never admit it to anyone. Not even to Nina; he'd be mortified if she ever found out.

He removed his iPhone from his pocket, scrolled down to contacts and sent a message to Lyla:

Safe at work. Karpov is a fucking nightmare. Miss you and love you! Xoxo

A notification popped up on the screen - Lyla usually replied quicker than Jessie's entire thought process - it was like she knew what to say before he even thought it:

Kick him in the balls! Curled up in bed with the new Hunter Shea. Fucking love him!

Jessie replied:

You can leave me for him if you promise to kiss me once a week. Love you more than your love for Hunter Shea. Gotta go! Speak soon! xoxo

He placed the phone back into his pocket and clicked on the Google Chrome icon. The old PC grunted. Slowly, like condensing rainwater, Google's search page opened up on the screen. Jessie liked keeping Google Search open in case he needed it during an emergency; not that there ever would be one, of course. The Murray building was an immortal piece of crap. Jessie laughed at the thought of a building being alive, shook his head and dialed Mrs. Rose's number.

CHAPTER THREE
5PM

Gloria Rose, aka *Mrs. Rose,* had moved into the Murray building back in '76.

It was a humid day, and her skin prickled from excitement. She had just started a secretarial job at her father's law firm and needed a place of her own. The Murray building towered above her like a Leviathan awoken from a deep slumber. She touched the fresh paint on the walls and smelled the scent of rosemary and sage.

The building was all over the front pages. It was a monolithic structure built by a wealthy businessman who had invested all of his cash into this concrete creature. Gloria reveled in the poshness of it all. Her apartment, number 46, was on the fifth floor; the views were poetic. Gloria could see the entire city from her window, stretched out like a slim man with a halo of sun around his head. It was, to Gloria, a magnificent sight.

She threw open the windows and danced on the couches. The rent was so low that she didn't even need to save. She could pay her rent and live a luxurious life without the need for stashing away her cash. She prayed silently to God that first night and thanked Him for giving her the ultimate abode. God had given her so much, and the Murray building was merely the icing on her blessed cake.

Gloria hosted raging parties filled with LSD and taut men with skimpy clothing. She slept with more than a dozen guys – and once even had a threesome. But, Gloria's hedonism came to a screaming halt during the early 80s when her job as Office Manager ended abruptly as her father's misdeeds came to light.

The whole nation reeled from what he had done; he'd used the Italian mafia's money to secure guilty verdicts for those individuals who tried to escape a life of crime.

He'd even dabbled in murder, paying off a hit man to assassinate a high-ranking defector. His trial was short and succinct. Forty years behind bars. Gloria wept for her father in court that day. Her mother had a nervous breakdown. The family lost everything, including their home in the Hamptons and their Sicilian villa. Gloria's father was murdered in prison a mere two months into his sentence, an obvious hit. Her mother, already fragile and broken beyond repair, jumped off a bridge and drowned in the icy river.

Gloria, the socialite and adored daughter of one of the most influential lawyers in the city, found herself without a job – and even worse, without an income.

Gloria used up all of her savings to pay for food, gas and rent. In 1997, a sweet, albeit gruffly Polish family moved into the apartment Nina now resided in. Gloria looked after their home when they were at work, becoming their glorified housekeeper. Until that fateful night when a gang leader entered the building, broke down the door and murdered the entire family, except for the daughter, Marita Merkovitz; also known as Nina Corletti's ex-BFF.

Not long after the massacre, Gloria received a letter from a Mr. Samuel Murray – the owner of the Murray building. He informed her that she could stay in the building forever and never worry about rent. Gloria cried like a child; God had saved her once again.

And it was that same God that brought Nina and Mia into her life. She felt a deep connection with both the girls, especially Mia. The child of circumstance was highly intelligent and read books well beyond her years. Gloria enjoyed looking after her – it gave her some zest for life again. And Gloria bathed in the sanctity of it all, she felt like her final good deed in life was to look after Nina and Mia at all costs.

Gloria realized she was reminiscing again when Mia touched her shoulder and asked for milk.

"Surely, my girl. A big glass of milk coming right up!" She went to the kitchen, poured the milk and handed it to a jolly Mia.

"Mommy is going to make pancakes when she comes back from work," Mia said.

"Is that so?" Gloria smiled.

The phone rang. Mia perked up like a kitten. Gloria lifted the receiver. It was Jessie doing his daily ritual – checking up on Gloria.

"How's it hanging, Mrs. Rose? You still old?"

"Jessie, my dear, I ate young men like you for breakfast back in the day. Don't let this old body fool you. What do you want?"

"The usual...how are you holding up?"

Gloria sighed.

"Well, except for Karpov's constant bitching, I am right as rain. Thank you, Jessie."

Jessie whispered, "He's a real shit today, Mrs. Rose."

"Don't let him get to you, kid. He's just a Russian without his vodka. How's the drug trade downstairs?"

"Two tweakers came in earlier and bought some stuff from him. We should seriously call the –"

"No! We'll all get kicked out, Jessie. Let the tweakers do what they have to do. Like my late husband used to say; 'Any economy is a good economy.'"

Gloria's late husband was a one-time affair. She met him at a party, they got married a month later and divorced two weeks after that. She liked being called 'Mrs. Rose' – it gave her an air of authority.

"Look, do you want me to come down and deal with Karpov?" Gloria asked.

"Nah. It's all okay, Mrs. Rose. Just..."

"Just what, Jessie?"

"Don't like drug addicts milling about. We've got kids and all kinds of people in this building. Is dangerous, you know?"

"As long as Karpov keeps them in the basement, I think we'll be fine."

"Thanks, Mrs. Rose. You have a good night, now."

"You too, Jessie."

Gloria placed the phone back on the receiver and turned her attention to Mia. The door to the hallway was slightly ajar. Mia was missing.

Gloria screamed.

5:15PM

Jessie ran down the staircase. "Mia! Mia!" he yelled her name. Where could she have gone? He checked every floor – nothing. How could a kid just up and leave like that?

Mrs. Rose was phoning the neighbors, trying to suss out whether they'd spotted a five-year-old Italian girl.

Jessie searched the entire building. He was out of breath and sweating like a kitchen on a restaurant's opening night.

How was he going to tell Nina that they lost her daughter?

"Only one place left to check," Jessie muttered under his breath. He flew down the main hallway and pushed open the door that led to the basement – Mr. Karpov's drug den. Jessie flipped down the stairs, taking two, three steps at a time. A television blared in the distance. Jessie could feel the sound reverberate on his skin. *Please God, let Mia be safe.*

Mr. Karpov's door was a solid hunk of metal. Jessie banged with his fists on the icy steel exterior. Within seconds, Mr. Karpov ripped open the door and stormed at Jessie. The kid flew back into the wall and bumped his head against a cabinet.

"Jesus Christ, Karpov!" Jessie yelled.

"Sorry. Thought you were bad men." Karpov shrugged and helped Jessie up.

"Have you seen Mia Corletti?" Jessie asked.

"The Italian girl?"

"Yeah."

"Yes. She is inside."

"What?" Jessie's internal organs shuffled around like a nervous chess player.

"She came here. I gave her lollipop." Karpov smiled with one crooked tooth.

"A lollipop?"

"Yes. What? You think because I am Russian, I kill little girls?"

Jessie couldn't wrap his brain around Karpov's *empathy* towards children. The man was a tweaked out, paranoid Russian.

"No. I don't –"

Karpov spat at Jessie's feet.

"*Poshel na khuy!*" Karpov swore.

Mia appeared at the door. She sucked on a lollipop. Her black bangs covered the top of her eyes. She smiled at Jessie.

"Mr. Karpov gave me a lollipop!" She twirled around in her yellow dress and hugged Mr. Karpov.

"Mia! Why did you leave Mrs. Rose's apartment? We've been worried to death about you!" Jessie sounded more hysterical than he wanted to be.

"Sorry, Jessie. But Mrs. Rose was busy on the phone with you, and I just wanted to come down and see what was going on. Mr. Karpov brought me here to his nice place and put on a *Dora the Explorer* DVD."

Karpov winked at Mia. She returned the deliciously infantile favor.

"You can't go roaming the building! Come on, Mia! Mrs. Rose is in a state. Jeez, kid!" Jessie felt his anger boiling like a plutonium rod at critical mass. Why was he so angry with Mia? She was only five.

Mia sniffled and burst into tears. Mr. Karpov grabbed her under the arms and placed her on his hip.

"No crying, Mia. You are good girl. I know this; I am Russian."

Jessie couldn't believe what he was seeing. The mad Russian was more sympathetic towards Mia's tears than to his anger and frustration with a lost child.

Karpov patted the little girl on the head and took her hand in his. "Jessie. Go work. I take Mia to Gloria."

Jessie simply smiled and nodded. It was the most bizarre thing he'd ever seen, Mr. Karpov and Mia walking hand-in-hand towards the elevator, completely oblivious to the hysterics that had surrounded her sudden disappearance.

Gloria hugged Mia for what felt like an eternity. She thanked Mr. Karpov and promised to bake him a pie. He left with a shrug and a smile – *one good deed, Gloria.*

"Mia, if you *ever* scare me like that again, I am going to tell your mother to send you to boarding school."

"What's *board* school?" Mia asked incredulously.

"*Boarding* school. It's a place children go to so they can learn discipline."

"Disciple?"

"*Discipline.*" Gloria laid emphasis on the word and spelled it out for Mia. "It means you learn how to *not* be naughty."

"Am I naughty?" Mia gulped down another glass of milk.

"Today you were! But you know what?"

"What?"

Gloria kneeled to be at Mia's height.

"You are the most beautiful little girl in all of the land, and I love you to bits and pieces – cross my heart and hope to *not* die."

The old woman hugged the little girl. A last speck of sunlight slunk through them and surrounded their embrace like a depiction from the Bible.

And then Gloria heard the shots.

CHAPTER FIVE
5:45PM

At first Jessie thought some juveniles were tossing crackers into the recycling bins. *Bang. Bang. Bang.* Loud, like expletives in church.

Mr. Karpov came out of his basement and stared at the front door. The glass stretched to the ceiling – two doors were placed in the middle like they'd been forgotten at the last minute. A crack formed in the glass. A minuscule, spidery web of shattered glass spread out like a virus, engulfing the reflections in the entryway.

Jessie stared at the formations; it was hypnotic. He knew something was about to give, but he couldn't move from behind the desk. He felt frozen, numb. What was happening? Why were people shooting in the streets?

"Oh Jesus..." Karpov whispered.

"What? What is it?" Jessie's hysterical voice cracked and squeaked.

"It's *them*..."

"Who? Karpov?! Who is it?" Jessie jumped from his seat and rushed to Karpov's side.

The Russian had obviously seen something outside, and Jessie couldn't face not knowing; he had to see what the Russian saw.

It was a sight more terrifying than death.

A group of twenty men dressed in suits and balaclavas stood outside the Murray building. Each carried an assault rifle, and they fired shots into the air, screaming every time a bullet left the barrel.

Who were they? What did they want?

Jessie turned on his heels and ran to the workstation. There was a panic button underneath the desk drawer which, when pressed, locked the doors of the building. He fumbled around for a few seconds until he felt a bump. *Yes!* He pressed the button. Nothing happened. He pressed it again.

And again.

And again.

The doors just weren't closing.

Jessie felt urine leave his bladder and soak his pants as the shots rang out. *Bang. Bang. Bang.* And suddenly Karpov held Jessie in his arms. The Russian clicked a remote button *on* in his hands. The doors whispered. *Click. Click. Click.* The locks threw themselves into the bolts like suicidal bridge jumpers. A metallic door slipped down from the roof and covered the entrance in one swift motion.

"It's okay. I know what to do." Karpov's voice sounded unsteady. Broken, almost. Jessie collapsed in the Russian's arms. The world around him shimmered and screamed as blackness enveloped him.

Karpov placed Jessie down on the floor. He grabbed a pillow from one of the waiting area couches and slid it underneath his head. Jessie was out. Gone. Like a flame without oxygen. Karpov had witnessed this before when he still worked for the KGB when people would faint from sheer terror. And what was more terrifying than twenty men with assault rifles banging down your door?

Karpov had dealt with these honchos before – and he beat them at their own game.

CHAPTER SIX
1997 - 9:50PM

Samuel Murray was a whisper thin man with elegant eyes and an affluent voice. He was the epitome of wealth, born and bred into money like a racehorse is sired for racing.

At the age of 25, Samuel had already amassed a fortune on the stock market. His father, Samuel Murray Snr, gave him $100,000 in 1970 and told him to make ends meet forever. So Samuel did. And he did so gloriously - by 1997, Samuel was worth over $1 billion.

He could do whatever he wanted. However, the money he earned over the years was tied up in his *coup de grace*; the infamous Murray building. Although he was a billionaire, Samuel couldn't exactly spend any money. And neither did he want to. His dream was to create a scientific experiment – some would call it a game – which would follow him into the grave; something so insane that the newspapers of the future would talk about it for decades.

Samuel also despised Jews. He was a pro-Nazi sympathizer and staunch supporter of Apartheid. In fact, he met the instigator of Apartheid, Dr. Hendrik Verwoerd, back when he was still a boy. The man inspired him so much that he carried his anti-Semitism proudly. Jews had to die, The Supreme Race was white, and gay people were an unnatural abomination – a botched piece of nature.

When Samuel found out that a Polish Jewish family moved into the Murray building, he immediately activated his own personal army – twenty ex-soldiers hooked on drugs, sex and rape. He paid them each a million dollars per month for both protection and *extermination.*

The gang of men, all suffering from PTSD and other assorted psychiatric ailments, arrived at the Murray building just before nine one Sunday evening. They didn't know which apartment the Polish family lived in, but they knew that Samuel would execute them if they didn't bring him their heads. So, they spread out like bacteria and entered the building dressed in white suits and balaclavas. A Russian even held the door for them and asked them how they were. He didn't find it odd that masked gunmen had just entered his building, it was as if he knew what was happening.

"What's your name?" the leader barked.

"You call me Karpov. I am Russian. Not afraid of you."

"Karpov...I knew a Karpov once. I fucked his wife." The leader turned towards Mr. Karpov and pressed the muzzle of his assault rifle against the Russian's head. "Now tell me, you fucking swine, where does the Merkovitz family live?"

Karpov winced. His eyes leaked tears that he didn't know he had. The leader steadied the rifle on his shoulder and pressed the muzzle so deep into Karpov's face that his nose almost cracked.

"I don't know," Karpov said.

"Oh? Is that so? Communist pig! Tell me which apartment they stay in, or I'm going to blow your fucking red communist brain into ten million pieces. Now! Fucker!"

Karpov turned his head away. He didn't want to see the nozzle light up and watch his brains explode. Death comes easier when one looks away.

The leader lowered the gun. He turned to his gang and instructed them to search the building – floor for floor. They quickly scurried away as their leader punched Karpov hard in the stomach. The Russian doubled over and vomited on the luminous green carpet.

"Listen to me, you pig." The leader cleared his throat. "If we don't find that family, I am going to murder you, rape your wife and eat your children. Don't fucking test me."

Karpov's thoughts immediately went to Kara and Kyrinka – his wife and four-year-old daughter. They lived in the basement because they had been brought to the States illegally. Karpov had to make a decision; either save the Merkovitz family, or give them away and save his own.

The leader helped him make a decision. "I know your wife and daughter are in the basement, you fat fuck. So don't even think about warning them. I'll tear your daughter's heart out, I swear to God!"

Karpov burst into tears. He shook and trembled like a terrorized shadow. *Not my child...* "Apartment 47." Karpov did it; h sold out the Merkovitz family. Oh Jesus, they were going to kill them all. What did he just do?

The leader growled into a radio. "Number 47. Exterminate. *Now.* Over." He turned to Karpov and removed his balaclava. Karpov shielded himself from the gang leader's face – if he knew who he was, he'd surely kill him.

"Now go. Kill! Kill! Kill!" Karpov screamed in emotional agony. The leader's face was a haunting reminder of war; the entire left side was one massive burn mark, his eyes appeared hollow and soulless. This was a creature from a nightmare – Karpov's nightmare. Was this real?

The leader spun around and headed directly to the basement door. Karpov chased after him, but the butt of the man's rifle shattered Karpov's nose. "No! No!" he screamed and bled and cried and pissed himself. His wife. His daughter. Their innocence. Karpov fell to his knees and wept like a lost sailor at sea; he couldn't stop the evil from infecting his home.

Two shots.

One for his wife, and one for his daughter.

The leader cackled after he fired the bullets. Karpov keeled over on his side and writhed like a newborn. Evil is always muffled by the sound of hope. And Karpov had no hope left. He just wanted to die, like his daughter and wife. He'd failed the only beauty he had left in his life.

The leader reappeared in the doorway to the basement, blood spattered across his horrific face; the blood of Karpov's family. He spoke, but Karpov only heard his own heartbeat thumping, out of tune with the universe.

"Are you listening, pig?" the leader yelled into Karpov's ear. "I said, I have a message from Mr. Samuel Murray, my boss and yours. Guess what? You won the lottery, you fat fuck!"

"Stay away from me!" Karpov spat.

"Mr. Murray always gives when he takes away. You might have lost a wife and a daughter, but you won a ticket straight to the gravy train." The leader tossed an envelope on Karpov's chest. Cryinng, the Russian flicked it open.

Dear Gregor Karpov

We've never had the opportunity to meet. But I've watched you carry my building on your shoulders, and I must say, you've done a stellar job. We had to kill your wife and daughter - it's the cycle of life. My mercenaries would have murdered them with or without your cooperation.

However, my dear Russian friend, now you receive the greatest boon of all - my secret plan for the building you so adore.

Oh, the future holds so much!

One day, when all is said and dead, you'll receive a special message containing a blueprint for my plans. If you follow the yellow brick road, the great Land of Oz awaits.

You will remain in my building until my plans come to fruition. If you dare to leave or run away, I shall murder every single tenant in the building. I shall also instruct my mercenaries to burn you alive and feed you to the pigs.

You have nothing to fear except fear itself.

Good night, and good luck, my communist whore!

Sincerely,

SAMUEL MURRAY

CHAPTER SIX
PRESENT DAY - 6PM

Nina liked listening to Neil Young when she felt down or depressed; she downloaded all of his music on her iPhone and went through a phase where she listened to it incessantly. She popped in her earphones and pressed *play*.

Her shift had ended early because she'd dropped an entire plate of seafood on a customer's lap. Randy, her boss, sent her home and took her pay to make up for the embarrassment and the loss of food. *Jesus, Randy...*

Nina took the back entrance of the Murray building when she didn't feel up to chatting with Jessie or, God forbid, Mr. Karpov. None of the other tenants knew about the entrance, Jessie had showed it to her one night when she slipped out for a cigarette and she'd been using it ever since. Plus, after the horrid encounter with the seafood, Nina wanted nothing more than a plate of pancakes and an episode of *Keeping Up with the Kardashians*.

Nina pushed open the door and slipped inside. A blast of cool air enveloped her like an ice queen's embrace. *Was Karpov cooking up meth again? Did the aircon break?* Nina shuddered. She slipped into the back of the entrance hallway and pressed the button for the elevator.

As she waited for the ancient transport to arrive, she noticed her Starbucks latte shaking and rippling, which reminded her of the T-Rex scene in Jurassic Park. Nina found it odd, as she didn't hear or feel anything unfamiliar, except for the aircon and her burning feet - high heels and waitressing do not go together - there was nothing that could create ripples in her damn coffee. *Jesus, Lord! Am I losing my mind?*

Then she heard it.

Clearly. Like a thunderclap on a damp summer's afternoon. Nina stopped the music and pulled out her earphones. She felt the blood stop in her veins. There were gunshots in the street. Assault rifles. *Rat-tat-tat. Bang.* Nina had fired one once, an ex-boyfriend had taken her to a shooting range for Valentine's Day; she almost shot him for being so stupid. Who goes shooting on the most romantic day of the year? He was a Republican, so that could have been it, that or he was just emotionally dead.

Dead.

"Oh God! Mia!" Nina felt a sudden urge to run up the staircase, grab Mia and flee the building. Death hung heavy in the air like a slain animal's rotten entrails. Was it war? What was going on? But, before Nina could find a rational reason why assault rifles would be rattling in the street, a large hand clamped down on her shoulder.

She spun around and instinctively kicked the person between the legs. She brought down her left fist and bashed it against her attacker's temple. A massive, looming shadow crashed to the floor. Nina took a moment to survey her surroundings. The attacker was down - she had to run.

"Good God, woman! You insane!" Karpov yelled from below. His accent sounded loaded with blood and shock. Nina gasped. How could she have not noticed Karpov?

"Oh my God! Mr. Karpov! I am so sorry. I thought you were -"

"You damn American women! Russia should have nuclear bombed you."

Nina bent down and helped Mr. Karpov up from his pained crouch. She dusted off his wife beater shirt, smiled meekly and exhaled all of the air in her lungs. "I am so sorry..." She was quite embarrassed, actually; Mr. Karpov was just an old man.

"You have to get to Mia. Big war coming. Lots dead. Please, Nina." Karpov grabbed her by the shoulders with both hands. Nina noticed tears streaming down his face. Was he actually crying? Nina stared at the old Russian for what felt like an eternity. Did he just tell her to fetch Mia because of impending war? Nina's instincts kicked in, and she hurtled towards the elevator.

"No! Take stairs!" Karpov yelled.

Without looking back, Nina swept through the door to the stairwell and ran up the staircase, leaving her high heels behind. She made it to the fifth floor. Her eyes darted around like she was on LSD. Mrs. Rose's apartment door was closed. Nina grabbed the handle and turned. Nothing. It was locked.

"Gloria! Mia!" Nina cried.

The bolts clicked, and the door swung open. Mrs. Rose appeared to be in a state of shock, her wide blue eyes held Nina like an ocean current. Nina knew fear when she saw it, and Mrs. Rose was long gone. Barely nodding to Mrs. Rose, Nina fled past the old woman and found Mia sitting on the kitchen counter.

"Mommy!" Mia jumped into her mother's arms.

"I'm here, baby. I'm here." Nina held her daughter tight as instinctively, she knew that neither of them would survive the night - the shocks of gunfire were coming closer with every second.

Nina knew the Murray building had housed some unsavory characters in the past. Perhaps this was just a tweaked out tenant with a massive drug debt? Perhaps the people with the guns would leave once they found their druggie? Nina prayed. She took a seat on Mrs. Rose's couch, Mia clutched tightly around her waist. She looked at Mrs. Rose - the door was still open, and the woman looked stunned, like a victim of PTSD.

"Gloria. What the hell is going on?" Nina asked.

"Hell, Nina. That's what's going on. The Devil is at our door, sniffing us out like we're pieces of meat."

Nina wasn't in the mood for a religious sermon. Something told her that she had to be aggressive and impatient.

"Gloria, I don't know what you're talking about, but if we're in danger, I need to know. We need to get to safety."

"We can't leave the building." Gloria sighed.

"What?"

"I said, we cannot leave the building. It's all in the plans. I never believed it. I thought it was all a lie...but no...Samuel knew what he was doing."

Nina, already impatient and agitated, barked, "Who is Samuel? What the fuck is going on?"

"That's a bad word, Mommy!" Mia squeaked.

"Do you know why I've lived here my entire life?" Gloria was busy pouring herself a glass of whiskey.

"Because of Mr. Murray? Your secret benefactor?"

Gloria gulped down the entire glass. She then tossed it to the side and drank straight from the bottle.

"He was the Devil. He kept me here, as a prisoner."

"Jesus, Gloria! Have you lost your mind?" Nina grabbed the bottle from Gloria's grip and poured out the contents in the sink.

"He told me I'd find out the truth...that one day I'd play his sick game...I thought it would never happen. But the gunshots prove otherwise."

"Gloria! Get it together! Where will we be safest? We need to hide. Now!"

"They'll find us...just like they found that poor Jewish family. I watched them do it, you know? I saw the terror on their faces as the bullets tore through their organs."

Nina shivered. She grabbed Gloria by the wrist and led her to the bedroom. She slammed the door shut behind her and instructed Mia to get into a closet. The little girl cried with terror.

"It's okay, sweetheart. I won't let anyone hurt you. Just hide in here for a little while so Mommy can keep us safe." Mia nodded and pulled the closet door shut behind her. Nina turned to Gloria and said, "Start talking. Tell me everything."

CHAPTER SEVEN
6:15PM

Maya and Kylie had been dating for three years when they decided to move in together. Both were 25 years old, and both worked at the Starbucks down the street; they were the fastest baristas in town, as one customer put it.

The couple ensured that their shifts coincided so they never missed a moment with each other. Maya, with her spiky blonde hair and collection of nose rings - which she took out for work - always told Kylie that she'd never met a girl like her. Kylie was the complete opposite of Maya; she being a voluptuous brunette with sharp green eyes and a penchant for the dramatic. The two of them just clicked.

Neither had any qualms about moving into the Murray building, where they lived two apartments down from Nina and her daughter. Maya loved giving Mia cookies when she saw her, the two had a special bond. Kylie, on the other hand, didn't like Nina or her daughter; she'd had an Italian girlfriend once, and it ended badly. Maya called it the *Lesbian Parable*.

They were asleep in bed when the first shots rang out. Kylie quickly got out of bed and rushed to the window. It seemed to her like some drug deal gone bad. Or a gang war. It was only when a stray bullet punched through their window when Kylie realized that they weren't safe. Maya scoffed at her and called her paranoid. Kylie phoned reception, but Jessie wasn't picking up, odd, because Jessie always answered the phone.

Always.

"Get back into bed, babe. We'll fix the window tomorrow," Maya said. She took a pillow and put it over her head to drown out the sound of gunshots. Kylie nibbled on her fingers. "Maya. Listen to me! This looks like something out of a war movie - it's just not right, okay?" Kylie grew exasperated with Maya's indifference.

"It'll all go away soon. They're just playing war games in the street. Don't stress about it," Maya groaned.

"I'm going downstairs. Jessie isn't answering the phone."

"Kylie, you can go, but I promise you that Jessie is most probably watching porn or something. Go, if it's going to make you feel any better. But I gotta sleep, babe. I'm knackered."

Kylie weighed up her options: go downstairs and check on the situation, or get into bed and sleep the fear off. No, the latter wasn't going to work; Kylie knew she'd be up pacing the apartment within less than ten minutes.

She quickly dressed in a tracksuit and a hoodie, took the apartment keys and headed downstairs. She remembered to lock the door - just in case someone murdered Maya in her sleep. *God, I'm so dramatic!*

The elevator pinged, announcing her arrival. The doors breathed open. Kylie stepped out and walked the entrance hallway towards Jessie's desk. She'd forgotten her shoes - the luminous green carpet tickled her feet.

Kylie immediately noticed the increase in gunshots. It went from *bang bang bang* to *rat-a-tat-tat-tat* - as if someone had fine-tuned the rhythm. As she came around the corner that led into the reception area, Kylie saw the steel door covering the entrance and followed the spidery webs of glass with her eyes.

Up, up, up.

"Jessie?" She called out. Something here was very, very wrong; Kylie felt the peculiarity vibrate in her chest.

Mr. Karpov stood by the entrance. His head was busted up and bleeding. He didn't notice Kylie until she was almost upon him. He turned his eyes towards her and sighed a deathly sigh. *What was going on?* She heard someone else groan; it was Jessie. He stood at the desk and held his head. His pants were soiled by urine.

"What in fuck's name is going on? Jesus! Jessie!" Kylie was terrified.

Jessie swiveled his head and stared at her for a moment. "Oh, hi Kylie. Yeah, shit's going down...sorry about my pants."

"Mr. Karpov? What happened to him? What's going on, Jessie? A fucking bullet tore through our apartment. We have to call the cops."

"You can't...I tried," Jessie said.

"What do you mean?" Kylie dialed 911 on her iPhone.

Your call cannot currently connect. Please check your signal and try again.

She dialed again. Same message. She tapped on the Facebook icon - *CONNECTION FAILURE.* She switched over to the Wi-Fi. Same message. Her phone was useless. Kylie felt the blood rush from her face - they were trapped and unable to communicate with the outside world.

"Signal jammers," Mr. Karpov spoke with an unsteady voice.

Kylie looked at him. Her mouth couldn't close - she was in shock.

"Wh-who is doing this?" she asked.

"The Devil. Bad man." Mr. Karpov struggled to speak without a loaded accent; it seemed heavier to Kylie than ever before.

"Let's go, guys. My car is outside. We can use that secret back entrance which Nina always uses." She glared at Jessie.

"We leave. We die," Mr. Karpov whispered.

"No, Mr. Karpov. Fuck this! I won't be kept prisoner in my own fucking apartment building!" Kylie spun on her heels and ran towards the back exit.

Jessie yelled at her to stop, but she was burning up pure adrenaline. The claustrophobia mounted - Kylie had to breathe. She had to get out. She had to see the stars. She had to. It was the only way.

Kylie half-kicked the back door. It swung open. The night smelled like oil and haunted seconds. She was out. She'd made it. No fucker was going to keep her inside – no, sir! Kylie headed for her car. It was less than twenty feet from the door. *Get to the car, open the door, climb in and drive.* "My fucking car keys..." Kylie had forgotten her only salvation. She just had to turn around and go get Maya. That was all. No need to get paranoid about mad gunmen roaming the street. Maybe it was a prank?

And then she felt it.

A burning hot gun muzzle pressed hard against the back of her head. They'd caught her.

She dropped everything, including the keys to her apartment. Instinctively, Kylie put her hands up in a show of surrender.

"Where you goin', Little Miss Piggy?" The gunman spoke like a cowboy, his voice was tough and roughened by years of cocaine abuse.

"N-n-nowhere. I just -"

"You just what? Huh? Thought y'all could take off in your shit hybrid car?"

Kylie's lips trembled. Tears streamed down her neck.

"No! I just wanted to check whether I locked my car. You know how bad the neighborhood is."

"Yeah? How bad is it?" He laughed.

"Well, it's not good. Look, I can just turn around and go back inside. You guys...I mean, you people..."

"Us people? What you sayin', bitch?"

The nozzle went in deeper. It buried itself in Kylie's hair. She could feel the gunman's breath on her neck.

"Sorry. I mean, you guys with the guns...you can do whatever it is you came here to do. I won't tell. I promise. I can't even phone 911, because the signal is blocked by something."

"We blocked it..." he whispered.

"Jesus...*please*! Just let me go back inside."

"Beggin' whore you are, ya know that?"

Kylie burst into hysterics. She cried so hard that every bone in her body shook.

The gunman grabbed Kylie by the back of her hoodie, spun her around and tossed her to the concrete like a forgotten rag doll. Kylie's hands scorched from the friction of concrete, blood trickled down her wrist. And her knee, oh God, her knee...it couldn't turn. A sharp, intense pain shot up her left leg and buried itself in her chest - she had broken her kneecap. A black boot came down on her hand. She screamed until she tasted copper as every finger snapped upon impact.

"You screamin' got me hard. And I ain't gettin' hard for a fat dyke."

The gunman slapped Kylie against the head. The hearing in her left ear went away and was replaced by a buzz. Bile rose in her throat – thenn she poured out her stomach's contents. It smelled bitter, like piss and pain and cancer. Her vision blurred. *He's going to kill me...*

The door to her left swung open. Mr. Karpov had a shotgun mounted in his massive arms.

"Step away. Or you die."

The gunman giggled. "Ooh! The communist pig has a shotgun! You gon' shoot me, you old fuck?"

"*Da.*"

The shotgun released a horrific chorus of scattered pellets. The gunman's suit ripped open. Blood leaked out of his chest. The balaclava stuck to his face as he mumbled an incomprehensible slew of words.

Kylie looked at the gunman. He staggered, dropped the assault rifle and dropped to his knees. The shotgun blast had ripped what remained of Kylie's hearing apart, so she didn't hear Mr. Karpov yelling at her to get up.

She stared down at her attacker's body, watching it smash into the concrete, bleeding everywhere. So much blood...the red river that erupted from the gunman's neck soaked Kylie's pants. She scuttled away, banging her busted knee against the sidewalk behind her. Kylie muffled a scream.

Jessie, eyes darting like fireflies, appeared behind Mr. Karpov. Although he was shocked by the brutal scene before him, his adrenaline urged him to rescue Kylie from her pitiable place in the car park. He grabbed her by the arm and straddled her on his back, saw that her hand was a mangled mess of bones and blood and shredded flesh.

Jessie heard footsteps. He hissed. Mr. Karpov held open the door. Jessie shook his head. He ducked down behind a car with Kylie on his back. Mr. Karpov's eyes bulged. Two gunmen came around the corner. The taller of the two yelled, "Carlo! Fuck! He's dead! Over here, guys!"

Sweat dropped from Jessie's forehead, ran down his nose and splashed on the concrete. It was dark outside, even with the countless fluorescent bulbs buzzing and ticking like an impatient audience clicking their tongues. The car park looked raw and rotten, a couple of cars, including Kylie's bright yellow hybrid and Mr. Karpov's white van, seemed lifeless. It was as if they'd never be driven again because their owners would be dead soon. And that felt like a *fact* in Jessie's mind. Not a theory. They were doing to die.

Another three gunmen rounded the corner. All of them wore the signature white suits that had terrified Karpov so many years ago. The Russian swiveled the shotgun to face the oncoming men, slipping into the door and leaving a crack open for the shotgun muzzle; if he was going to shoot, he had to stay protected. The old man's hands trembled. He exhaled slowly. This was it.

The gunmen were edging closer to the dead one they called Carlo. Jessie and Kylie were less than two feet away from them. One squeak or creak, and it would be over. Karpov prayed that Jessie and Kylie wouldn't be found. *God, I know I don't speak to you often, but please help Jessie and Kylie. You took my wife and child, the least you can do is to save the two kids.*

His prayers were short-lived.

One of the gunmen, a short, stocky figure, walked towards where Jessie and Kylie hid. He almost tripped over his own two feet when he found them. He called over for the others to come "claim their prize".

All five gunmen closed in on Jessie and Kylie. Jessie closed his eyes and breathed sharply, his heart thumping around in his chest like a wild horse. Kylie mumbled something incoherent; so this is how they were going to die - gunned down in a car park behind a crappy old building that no one liked. This is how it was going to end...

Jessie said a couple of prayers. He slowly removed Kylie from his back. She slid down the side of the car. Blasts of blood clung to her chin, knee and arms. Jessie wished he could have saved her. If only he had moved quicker.

One of the gunmen removed his balaclava. Before Jessie looked away, he spotted a glimpse of his killer: a tall, washed out face with hollow red eyes and a thin smile. A purposeful smile. A destined smile.

"Don't have to look away, kid. You *are* going to die whether you saw my face or not." The gunman's voice lilted at the end, indicating a British heritage.

Jessie turned to him and said, "I don't know your name or your past...but think before you kill me. How can you gun down a 19-year-old black kid from the Bronx? Dude. I have a life to live." Jessie's voice was heavy, his feeble attempt at changing the gunman's mind merely incensing the others. They also pulled off their balaclavas - a sea of shaved heads and haunted eyes, a menagerie of alcoholic lips, a string of veins carved up by years or heroin - if Jessie weren't so afraid, he'd have found the scene serene.

He eyed each one as they looked at him with pity and a hint of contempt. Jessie stepped out from underneath the car park awning. He looked up at the stars. For less than a nanosecond, Jessie could *feel* the planet hurtle around the sun, churning lava beneath the crust as it spun and spun and spun. *This is beautiful,* Jessie thought. *And now I bid you farewell...*

The semi-British gunman whipped out a 9mm pistol. He pushed it against the back of Jessie's head. The gun was locked and loaded. He could just pull the trigger and watch the black kid's brains spill out on the concrete. But something moved in the corner of his eye and he hesitated. He didn't look towards the movement, as he was trained not to give away his position.

A sudden flash of light blinded him, a thousand pinpricks popped on his face. *Crackle. Crack. Crack. Pop.* The gunman thought it was fire at first. He rubbed his eyes, and instead of feeling his eyelids, he felt his raw, wet eyeballs. His fingers creeped around his cornea, dipping in and out of the fleshy hollow just beside the eye. Why couldn't he feel anything? Why couldn't he see what was going on? Someone grabbed him by the throat. He thought it was a person, but no, this was stronger than any man's deadly grip; it was a wet vine that curled around his aorta and tugged at his brainstem.

Jessie heard the gunshot and thought it was the end. But no, he was still standing. He quickly scanned his body for any pain. Nothing. He turned around. The British gunman's face was contorted and split down the middle. Three holes lined his left cheek, his eyes were bleeding, and a spot of blood blossomed on his neck.

Jesse realized that the gunman was digging and scratching at his own eyes, then a small fountain of blood squirted from the tiny hole in the gunman's neck. Jessie heard more shots. He watched as the four gun muzzles splashed the dark with rigid light. *One. Two. Three. Five. Ten. No, more. Fifty. A hundred.* Jessie mentally counted the shots. He couldn't keep up. Nor could he feel his legs. Why were they numb? And why did his knees explode a split second ago? Jessie's heartbeat thumped and pounded like a thing posessed And then he felt his heart stop.

It stopped in his ears, in his chest, in his fingertips. How could anyone live without a heartbeat? Jessie thought.

And then he stopped thinking.

Forever.

EVEN THOUGH KYLIE WAS all but beyond repair - busted knee and a mangled hand - she still managed to crawl underneath her car. There, she curled up into a fetal position and watched as Mr. Karpov shot the gunman who was positioned behind Jessie. She felt the air ignite when the remaining four gunmen decided to unleash all hell on Jessie's body, tearing apart the kid's entire torso.

Kylie looked away, closed her eyes. There was nothing she could do for him. He was dead. The gunmen wanted revenge, they were incensed and adamant and evil and oh god, her knee pained and her hand - her lovely hand - hung from her wrist like a slaughtered pig in an abattoir.

Why did she come down here? Couldn't she have listened to her Maya? Why was she always so stubborn? Maya was right, Kylie should have stayed away. But now it was too late. Death was around the corner, knocking on Kylie's door like some blood-crazed Jehovah's Witness.

Beep. Click.

Kylie's car was being unlocked. Someone had her keys. Oh God...Maya! The car hummed to life above her head - the engine was about to fire up. Kylie crawled away as quickly as she could, pulling herself from beneath the car. But, before she could move her legs out of the way, the hybrid rolled back. Kylie heard her own bones shatter as the wheels rolled over her legs.

Pop.

Pop.

Pop.

Each pop heralding another shattered shard of bone bursting through Kylie's skin.

She had never felt so much pain, it was so unbearable that she vomited and pissed herself. The car revved. Once. Twice. Kylie looked down at her legs - two mangled, bloodied stumps on the black concrete, with loose bones sticking out of her feet.

The hybrid's headlights switched on, momentarily blinding Kylie. Where did the gunmen go? Who was in the car? Kylie dipped her head and hoped for it all to just go away.

Unconsciousness enveloped her in its humble embrace.

CHAPTER EIGHT
7PM

Ben Sussman – or *Benji*, as his kids called him – knew he had to steer his team into the Murray building before 8pm; time was running out.

Mr. Murray had given strict instructions: *eliminate, exterminate,* and *explode.* The elimination part was easy – target the lower floors first, eliminate the strongest. Then exterminate – simply go through the building and murder everyone on sight. And finally, explode – plant the explosives as strategically as possible, press the red button at 6am.

This final phase was the easiest; once the building went down in flames, Ben and his team would receive a cool $100 million for their efforts.

None of the tenants were even remotely capable of stopping them. Ben's team were born and bred mercenaries – men with tough pasts and horrid lives. Ben – *Benji Babe,* to his lawyer wife – had been the leader of Samuel Murray's personal army since the early nineties; he was the one who shot and killed Gregor Karpov's family. Oh, how the old man's wife looked when the bullet blew out her brains... quite exquisite.

Omnipotent. Religious, Ben lived in a cushy apartment on the Upper West Side with his wife and two daughters. They thought he was a handyman, in fact no one knew about his real job – that of an assassin. To everyone he knew, he was just Ben, the Army vet with the burned face and the kooky personality. But to his team, he was Benjamin Sussman, ex-Special Ops, mean and tougher than Satan himself. He was the man who murdered, raped and pillaged; Ben was *The Viking*.

Out on the street outside the Murray Building, Ben smiled at his thoughts. He was content, because tonight was the end of the road. After Samuel Murray had passed away the previous day, Ben had finally opened the legal letter that the old boy had given him upon being appointed.

Benjamin Daniel Sussman

I, Samuel Edward Murray, hereby invoke the War Game. You, as leader of my army, will call your brothers in arms exactly 24 hours after my death.

You will proceed to my building; you will eliminate, exterminate and plant special explosives in certain parts of the structure.

Gregor Karpov and Gloria Rose are the only two tenants who will become aware of my plan. It's their decision whether they share it with others or not.

The rules are simple:

If ONE (only one) tenant eliminates you and your team, they will receive a total sum of $100 million at 6am the following day.

If you and your team (dependent upon how many remain) manage to exterminate everyone in the building and blow it up, at 6am the following day, a total sum of $100 million will be divided up amongst you.

If a tenant escapes during your assault, no one receives anything; it is your job to ensure that no one leaves the building. I have instructed my wife to manage the War Game after my passing. She will assist you with signal blockers and an armory. If anyone tells a lie about the assault and/or rearranges the details of the night, all of you will be executed immediately.

Do not create your own narrative, soldier.

Beat the War Game.

Or die trying.

Good night, and good luck, my monstrosity.

Sincerely,

Samuel Murray

BEN ROUNDED THE CORNER at the back of the building. He heard shouts and shots, and the noise irritated him. It was time to breach the building and begin the Game; money was on the line here – a literal fuckload of money. Ben would be able to afford a face transplant with his share of the prize!

Ben watched as a yellow hybrid reversed into the back wall. The front and rear windshields screamed as they exploded into little particles; a storm of glass snowflakes raining down upon the concrete.

The fluorescent bulbs spat and sputtered near the car park's awning, illuminating a woman missing her legs who lay unconscious and bleeding – or dead in the space where the hybrid used to be. *Fucking Christ! Someone destroyed her legs. Bad drivers...*Ben giggled. He imagined the woman waking up without legs and asking someone to put them back on; why was the most gruesome scenario always Ben's favorite place to go?

Simple – the scene before him captured the ghoulish attention of his *serial killer* imagination.

Aside from the fat girl with bloodied stumps for legs, Ben could see five of his men and a black kid strewn around the car park like jack-o-lanterns at a Halloween orgy.

Whoever was driving the hybrid would be dead soon, so Ben shifted his focus to the slightly ajar back entrance door; there was something sticking out.

Ben, trained in stealth and silence, slithered into the shadows, scurried down the wall of the building (the broken, stuttering fluorescent lights hid him after every second step), and slumped behind the cracked door. A shotgun stuck out through the narrow gap, which Ben found quite bizarre – was someone actually hiding in there?

He knocked. "Pizza delivery. Open up!" As if someone would be all, *thank God for pizza – let's stop the murdering and eat.* Ben giggled again and the shotgun slid back inside like a scared spider.

The remaining men – fifteen left now – including Ben, were on the other side of the building and well out of his way – planting the explosives. Ben knew that he would eventually have to kill his comrades – \$100 million can make a man quite greedy. But before any of that, he had to first figure out what needed his attention more – the girl without her legs, the driver in the hybrid, or the stupid fool with the shotgun?

He glanced over at the legless girl. She wasn't moving, most likely dead already. The driver sitting in the hybrid lay on their side, slumped over the dashboard. The shotgun-wielding maniac had retreated into the building when he – was it a he? – heard Ben's supposedly witty quip about pizza.

"Who should I kill first, hmm?" Ben muttered. "The legless bitch? The stupid driver? Or the shotgun fucker? You guys...it's so hard to choose. The one without the legs...perhaps I could persuade her to suffer a bit more? Fun, fun, fun!" Ben smiled to himself; it was the most fun he'd had since raping the blonde chick who worked at the gas station.

The legless woman groaned. She was still alive! Even more fun for Ben. He left the back door and walked over to where she lay. The scene was a gruesome reminder of what happens to piggies who don't learn. Streaks of flesh and blood lay stretched out behind her, a couple of pieces of bone had been dragged across the lot by the driver in the hybrid. Their off-white color reminded Ben of shark's teeth – wild slices from nature's most ruthless predators.

"Hi, little piggy! What would your name happen to be?" Ben asked as he kneeled by her face.

"H-h-help me…" Kylie spat out a gob of blood – it landed on Ben's shoes. He thanked her by slapping her across the face. She jerked backwards.

"I asked your name…and then you went and ruined my shoes. Not a nice little piggy, are we?"

"Geddaway from me…"

"What's that?" Ben cocked his rifle.

"You…you are evil." Kylie turned her head away.

"Oh, yes, I am, my dear. I am the reaper." Ben pushed the assault rifle into Kylie's mouth. The barrel scraped her tongue and cracked a few teeth. Ben loved to see the horror on people's faces just before they died; this one was beautiful, although she barely cried. He jerked the assault rifle in her mouth, bashing out a handful of teeth. She gagged, groaned and sighed.

"Now why don't I fire off a couple of shots? It'll blow your mind!" He laughed. "Get it? Of course you do!" Ben patted Kylie's head.

"Get. The. Fuck. Away. From. My. Girlfriend." Maya's face, ruined by glass shards from the hybrid's windshield appeared behind Ben.

Maya had planned to have Kylie jump into the car and flee with her, but she had accelerated when she'd felt the vehicle bumping over something. She'd known at that moment that she'd driven over the love of her life.

Furious and hysterical, Maya had punched the accelerator with her foot, spinning over Kylie's legs and crashing into the wall behind the car park. She'd also mown down four of the gunmen. Maya had wanted the smash to kill her, but it hadn't. Instead, it had just stunned her, so Maya had pretended to be dead when she saw the gunman lurking round the corner.

Luckily, Maya had grabbed a butcher knife from the kitchen before she'd raced downstairs. She knew she was up against assault rifles, but if she could surprise one or two of the killers, at least she'd go out with a bang.

Ben spun his head around. He laughed. "God damn...you two are *dykes*? You look like one, but not Legless Lisa over here. How long have you been together?"

"None of your fucking business. Step away from her, or I'm going to stab you in the fucking throat!" Maya held the knife in her right hand. She twirled it around, stabbing into the air above Ben's head. He simply ducked, even though the blade grazed the top of his head once or twice.

"What are you trying to do, bitch?" he asked Maya. She stabbed again. Ben ducked twice, ripped the assault rifle from Kylie's mouth and punched it hard into Maya's stomach. He fired off four shots and the muffled sound of organs exploding made Ben feel invincible.

The same couldn't be said for Maya; she doubled over, her face was a mass of confusion. She tilted her head to the side, as if asking Ben why he just did what he did.

"No! Oh God!" Kylie managed to moan.

Maya fell to her knees, blood pouring from her nose and lips. Her spiky blonde hair was rouge now – the bullets had exited her back and spewed blood all over her neck and head. She crumpled into a small ball of human flesh. Dead. Bleeding.

Ben smirked. "Now your dyke girlfriend is all dead. God, that must be so hard for you?" he asked Kylie.

"I'm...going to get...you."

"No, little piggy. You're *not* going to get me. You're going to die. I'm thinking of leaving you to bleed out, but you seem like a crazy bitch. If you crawl away into the darkness, I don't get paid. And we can't have that."

He pulled Kylie's hair backwards, her head tilted until her throat went white. She groaned. Mumbled something. Ben knew his comrades would be almost done with setting the explosives, so he had to move quickly, he couldn't waste any more time. In one fell swoop,

Ben pressed the assault rifle against Kylie's exposed neck, pulled the trigger once.

Twice.

He laughed cheerfully when Kylie's head rolled away.

CHAPTER NINE
7:15PM

Nina, Mrs. Rose and Mia were locked in the bathroom. Nina knew it was the safest spot; if an intruder came in, she'd be able to get him before he got them. She held a small pistol in her trembling hands. Mrs. Rose gave it to her. Nina knew guns were lethal, but the tiny pistol didn't seem to adhere to the same theory. It looked like a pellet gun, which angry teenagers use to shoot birds.

Mrs. Rose and Nina watched the horror unfold in the car park. They sat on the windowsill in the bedroom. Nina cried when Jessie got shot; she had seen plenty violent movies, but she never thought someone's body could be ripped apart like that by bullets.

And when Maya - the sweet one - drove over Kylie's legs and crashed into the wall, Nina vomited on Mrs. Rose's bed. Mrs. Rose found a bottle of vodka in her cupboard and downed it, while Mia hid in the cupboard until her mom told her to come out.

Nina memorized the letter Mrs. Rose had received from Samuel Murray all those years ago.

Dear Gloria

My name is Samuel Murray. I am the owner of the building you currently reside in. After your father's misdeeds, it came to light that his only daughter was jobless and poor, unable to pay the weekly rent.

I am here to change all that.

You will not pay rent anymore. Instead, you'll stay in the building for the rest of your life. Upon my death, sometime in the future, I want you to read the following:

War Game by Samuel Murray

Gloria, you were chosen by me to keep this secret sealed until the day you heard gunshots from the street. This will be a sign that I am indeed dead and that my army of mercenaries have activated the War Game.

ONE (only one) tenant must survive the night. If you, or someone else, eliminate my men before 6am, the surviving tenant will receive a total sum of $100 million.

If my mercenaries survive, a total sum of $100 million will be divided up amongst the ones who remain.

They are instructed to strategically place explosives in the building - at 6am, one of them will press a button - this will take down the Murray building within seconds.

If someone escapes during the assault, no one will receive anything. If you alert the authorities, my men will blow up the building immediately. You won't be able to contact anyone - they will cut the landlines. And, if technology persists, they will also receive a signal blocker, in case one of you tries to use a Sat phone or one of those bulky mobiles. It'll block the signal.

You may keep this information to yourself, or you may share it with someone in the future. However, you must *remember that only ONE TENANT can survive. If there's more than one, someone will die randomly.*

If you decide to move away, I shall instruct my team to find and execute you.

You are now my prisoner, and my secret.

Good night, and good luck, my little bitch!

Sincerely,

Samuel Murray

"IF WE PULL THE FIRE alarm, we could get all of the building's tenants together," Nina said. Gloria considered this intently - the vodka had taken away all rational thought.

"But then they'll just kill everyone," Gloria said with a lisp.

"How many people live in this building? Do you know?" Nina asked a delirious Gloria.

"Fucked if I know, and I've lived here since God created Eden."

Mia gasped.

"Language, Gloria. I know you're drunk, but tone it down a bit - for Mia's sake?" Nina got up from the tiled floor of the bathroom.

"Oh." Gloria burped. "Sorry, Mia. Fu - I mean, *fudge...*"

"I've never met all the tenants. It's weird when I think about it now, but why is this damn building always so quiet and devoid of life? Are there any other tenants except those lesbian girls?"

"Watson. She lives on the third floor. A fat woman with a kind face. Gave her a pie once...bitch didn't even acknowledge me."

"Gloria! Language!"

Mia giggled.

"Oh." Gloria waved her hand in the air. "There's also Ken...strange one, that. He usually has young boys over...teenagers."

"Drugs, maybe?" Nina questioned her own question.

"No, he's most probably a pedophile." Gloria burped again.

"Mommy? What's a *peedoughfile*?" Mia was curious. Nina scratched her head. She wished Gloria would get sober.

"It's someone who likes dough. And files," Nina whispered. "A kind of businessman." Nina cringed at the thought of a businessman fiddling with young boys.

"Should we go get him?" Gloria asked.

"Ken?"

"No, Nina. Jesus. We should go get Jesus."

Nina didn't appreciate Gloria's drunken sarcasm. She was such a bitch!

"Remind me to never go into the Apocalypse with you. You're such a b!"

"What's a b?" Gloria asked.

"Never mind. Where does Ken stay?"

"Second floor. Apartment 24."

"Mia, will you stay with Mrs. Rose for a bit while Mommy goes out?" She hugged her daughter as she said this.

"Mommy! The bad men will get you!" She started crying like a banshee with hormone problems.

"Shh! Mia! Your mom has to go get Mr. Ken." Gloria clasped her hand around Mia's mouth. Nina, startled at the old woman's archaic form of child censorship, batted her hand away. It was instinctive. Gloria pulled her arm into her jacket and gasped.

"I'm sorry!" Nina knew she had temper, but hitting Gloria was perhaps the last thing on her life agenda; she was like family.

"Just go. Get out!" Gloria unlocked the bathroom and hustled Nina outside. She slammed and locked the door before Nina could protest. Nina's face was red with embarrassment. She sighed.

AFTER NUMEROUS WEIRD turns, Nina finally arrived at Ken's apartment. How had she never visited the second floor before? The Murray building was much like The Overlook Hotel - a labyrinth of madness and Shelly Duval's nervous breakdown all rolled into one.

Nina cleared her throat. She knocked twice. "Ken? My name is Nina Corletti. I live on the fifth floor. Are you here?" Nina knew to keep her voice down, but if she had the opportunity to gather tenants like a herd of sheep, she sure as hell wasn't going to abide by the Murray's rules.

Ken's door squeaked open. A young guy with listless eyes, bronze skin and a bulging six pack stared back at Nina. "Who the fuck are you?" he asked.

"Hi! Uhm, my name is Nina Corletti. I live on the top floor?"

"Listen, lady, I don't know what the fuck is going on outside. I just want to do my job and get out of here before a fucking drug deal goes bust."

Nina frowned.

"*Listen, dude.* I don't know who the fuck you are, but I know what's going on outside. You are going to die before the night is over. If we can -"

"Who's at the door, baby?" A male's voice rolled into Nina's ears. He sounded old. What was this young boy doing with an old man?

"It's an old lady from upstairs, Kenny!" the guy yelled.

"Mrs. Rose?" Kenny asked from within the apartment.

"No. Nina something."

"Corletti," Nina corrected him.

"The chick with the kid? The one I'd go straight for?"

Nina smiled. A gay man was willing to go straight for her. How charming!

Kenny came from behind the young kid and edged the door completely open. He was a tall man with dark eyebrows and wild hair; he looked more like a marijuana life coach than a pedophile.

"Oh, darling! To whom do I owe the pleasure of meeting a real Italian woman tonight?" Kenny stretched out his hand. Nina shook it slightly. She felt the urge to curtsey.

"Funny. Listen, Kenny - may I call you Kenny? - there's crazy shit going down outside. If you and your..."

"Boyfriend?" Kenny interjected.

"Boyfriend, yes. Well, if you two could come with me? I'm hiding in Gloria Rose's apartment with my daughter. I know what's going on...and I promise you that *you will die* if you don't listen to what I have to say."

Kenny's mouth hung open. His young boyfriend pouted. Nina had many gay friends, but these two were just all too stereotypical. What the hell...

"Are we in any danger? Brad and I have heard the shots - I even heard a shotgun go off a couple of times. We thought it was just Mr. Karpov protecting his turf."

Brad. Clichéd.

"It's way worse than a drug deal gone bad...there's about fifteen - five dead now - gunmen outside wearing white suits, balaclavas and carrying assault rifles. They've also rigged the building with explosives."

Kenny laughed. "Are you serious right now? Did Billy prank me? I swear to God -"

"Listen! Kenny! I don't know who Billy is. This is not a fucking prank! It's a reality game show gone horribly wrong." Nina grew frustrated; she didn't want to stand out in the open for so long. What if a gunman came down the hallway? He'd shoot them all to pieces.

Kenny scratched his head. "A reality television game show? Is it like *Real Housewives?*" Kenny was clearly not taking it seriously. Nina groaned.

"Kenny...come with me, or stay here. Your choice. I have to get back to my daughter." Nina crossed her arms.

"Okay, we'll come along for the ride. Brad, babe, get my *Evian*, will you?"

Several minutes later, Nina, Brad and Kenny arrived at Gloria's apartment. She opened the door and led them inside. "Charming..." Kenny muttered.

"Read this." Nina handed him Gloria's letter from Samuel Murray. She knew it was a dangerous move - what if Kenny and Brad tried to kill them for the money? But she had no choice. She *had* to help as many people as possible.

Kenny scanned the letter. Once. Twice. Thrice. He shook his head.

"This can't be real..." he whispered.

"It's real, Kenny." Nina placed a hand on his shoulder. He flinched slightly, looked into Nina's eyes and smiled warmly. Brad nodded when he read the letter. "I always knew Mrs. Rose was stuck in this place!" He proclaimed loudly. Kenny laughed, and even Nina had to smile.

The bathroom door opened. Gloria and Mia stepped out into the living room, the old woman clutching Mia's hand. She greeted Kenny and Brad, took another swig from the vodka bottle and slouched on the sofa.

"I think she's a bit drunk..." Kenny whispered with one hand covering the side of his face.

The night was merely beginning - God only knew what horrors they still had to face.

CHAPTER TEN
8PM

Ben and his gang of murderous madmen breached the building at exactly 8pm. *On time,* Ben thought. They worked the reception area, scanning for any hidden tenants or scared housewives. Nothing; the building's entrance was emptier than space. "Where the fuck is everyone?" Ben asked out loud.

"Hidin'," Jeremy said. Ben knew Jeremy from his childhood. The poor guy had been subjected to sexual abuse when he was a teenager and then sent to the Army to atone for his sins - now he was addicted to heroin and rape.

"The ten of you, including Jeremy," Ben waved his rifle over their heads, "go upstairs and start knocking on doors. If someone opens, shoot them in the face. Don't leave any prisoners. And those of you who like raping? Now's not the time. We gotta work. Go!"

Ten gunmen, including Jeremy, shuffled out of the reception area. Ben and the remaining four made a silent beeline for Gregor Karpov's basement apartment. Ben had a feeling Gregor was the one with the shotgun, so they had to be careful.

The five gunmen entered the concrete hallway that led to Gregor's apartment. Ben used two fingers to point at Gregor's apartment door. They couldn't make a sound, if the old Russian heard them, he'd start blasting away with his shotgun. Plus, Gregor knew the Murray building better than they did. He had an advantage.

The apartment door stood ajar. Ben used his rifle to creak it open. A television stood in the corner next to a dead green sofa. Some kind of reality show was on the screen, but the television was muted, so Ben didn't even bother to see what it was about. His men quickly cleared the apartment, shouting "Clear!" when they finished checking a room.

"Where is the communist pig?" Ben asked no one in particular. "Gregor! My friend. Where are you?" No sound. *He must be hiding*, Ben thought.

A POLICE CRUISER ARRIVED at the entrance to the Murray building. Lindsey Moss, who graduated from the police academy less than six months ago, had been busy patrolling the streets when she'd received the call about a noise complaint in the Murray building area.

The building was situated in the industrial outskirts, there were a couple of smaller buildings in the area that held no more than 50 tenants, and the rest was a deserted mess - factories in disrepair, car parks with broken, abandoned vehicles, alleyways that stank of meth and sex. The Murray building was feared by almost everyone on the force. Not only was the place an imposing monstrosity, it also carried with it the weight of decades of decay; it was just part of the cycle of abuse that New York offered its denizens.

Lindsey's blonde hair and blue eyes made for a perfect combo in the land of anti-Semitism. Her petite figure, blessed with voluptuous breasts, carried itself like some lithe vixen from a *film noir*. From the deserted street, she noticed the steel sliding door blocking the entrance to the building.

Lindsey felt a chill speed down her spine like an electric bolt, her instincts telling her something was very off with the situation. Slowly, she retreated back to her car so she could call in backup.

"Don't move. I shoot." A voice rumbled out of the darkness. Lindsey grabbed her gun and spun around to face the person who threatened her. There was no one. A scream followed by a piercing *rat-tatatatata* bled from the building.

Lindsey winced.

"Come out with your hands above your head! Drop the gun!" she yelled into the darkness. Suddenly, hard, heavy hands curled around her neck. A shotgun - Lindsey recognized it in an inastant, since she used to hunt with her father as a teenager - pressed against her spine.

"I can't." The accent was heavy. Russian?

"Don't do this...I'll drop my gun." Lindsey tossed her gun into the street. "Please don't shoot an unarmed officer. I beg of you."

The shotgun dug deeper. Lindsey's insides swirled around. She was terrified. *Swallow the fear,* she thought. *Just swallow the anger and the fear, Linds.*

"What do you want?" she asked the shotgun wielding Russian.

"Leave here. Let it go. No harm."

"Sir, I can't just -"

A sound from nearby cut off Lindsey mid-sentence. It was a man's voice - he was calling for help. The shotgun went higher up and brushed against Lindsey's neck. The man's fingers curved around her throat. *Strangulation?* Lindsey's biggest fear was being strangled to death.

The bile rose in her throat like a lazy murder of crows.

BEN WAS QUITE TAKEN aback by the blue and red lights. He immediately knew it was a police vehicle, but how could that be? No one in the building had access to a working phone – so how could they possibly phone the police?

Ben tuned into the police scanner he carried with him. It was a simple noise complaint. That meant one rookie cop and a bonus kill for Ben.

When he saw Gregor Karpov push the shotgun into the cop's back, he knew he had to contain the situation before she messaged for backup. He called out, "Help! Someone help me!" The cop's ears perked up and he knew he had her attention. If she left, Ben knew he would have no choice but to trigger the explosives, and God only knew what would happen to him and his team if they ended the mission prematurely. Yes, it was a failsafe, but what would it exactly mean? Would they get nothing? Would someone execute them?

He cut the lights to the ground floor. The once dimly lit reception area swallowed the darkness like an arsenic-happy Nazi. Ben ordered his men to switch on their night vision helmets.

"If anyone comes through that door, you shoot the holy fuck outta 'em! Acknowledge!"

"Acknowledged!" His men spoke in unison. They gathered around the back door like prowling panthers. Each assault rifle was aimed at the back entrance. *Any moment now*, Ben thought.

"WHAT'S YOUR NAME?" Lindsey asked the man with the shotgun.

"Gregor Karpov. You?"

He was Russian.

"Lindsey Moss. My friends call me Linds."

Karpov lowered the shotgun slightly. He didn't intend to kill the cop - he just needed her to leave. Get help. Yes, they'd blow the building, but at least they wouldn't be subjected to Samuel Murray's sick *War Game*.

"Do you need assistance, Gregor?" Lindsey asked tentatively.

"No. Go back to the police. Leave. Before you get hurt."

"What makes you think I'll get hurt if I go inside now?"

"I know." Gregor grunted.

"If you keep your shotgun on me, perhaps we could go around back and I can just peek inside?"

"What?" She knew she'd annoyed him.

"I'm not armed. You can lead the way. Take me so I can peek inside and see if anyone is hurt."

Gregor grunted again.

"No. You carry Taser? You shoot me. You die."

Lindsey feigned sympathy.

"No! Not at all. I'll help you. I promise."

Karpov shook his head. He couldn't risk it. But before he could make a decision, Lindsey swung around, grabbed the shotgun and smashed the butt into his face. She held the gun aloft, pointed at him. She needed one moment of weakness. And she found it. Just waiting there, like a broken down truck on the interstate.

"Get down on your knees! I won't ask again! Now!"

Gregor held his nose. Lindsey could see the blood boiling out of the injury. She felt no remorse - only instinct and fear. He went down on his knees and put his hands behind his head. Lindsey had him. She could call for backup and get the situation sorted out.

She walked to her cruiser, but as she bent down to get the radio, a bullet whispered past her and carved a sparkling hole into the dashboard, shattering the radio. Lindsey grabbed for the radio that hung over her shoulder, but yet another bullet stopped her in her tracks.

A huge hole formed near her clip-on radio, the hand piece ripped to pieces - as was Lindsey's shoulder.

She screamed.

With one hand, Lindsey spun the shotgun around to face the gunman. She fired off two shots before her ammunition was expended. Gregor stormed the cop, punching her in the throat and grabbing at the shotgun. Lindsey's vision became blurry; the Russian had a strange smile on his face.

Oh God...I am going to die tonight.

"Don't die!" Gregor howled. He threw his body onto hers and they both crashed to the sidewalk like tripped-up lovers.

Lindsey felt the hole in her chest growing wet. She smelled copper and gunshot residue. The Russian, an old man with heavy eyebrows and kind, albeit tough eyes stared down into her face. He begged her not to die. He was crying. She smelled his sweat - it poured out of him, the stick making her nostrils flare and bloody bile creep into her mouth.

Lindsey vomited, bloodied green stuff choked out of her. Her hands were cold. Frozen almost. How could that be? It wasn't cold outside...was this what dying felt like? As Lindsey finished her final mortal thought, three bullets pierced her brain.

Gregor shrieked.

At least she'd died quickly; he consoled himself, not like the others who had to suffer first.

Gregor kissed the dead cop on the forehead and wailed like a Sicilian mourner.

"SO, MY COMMUNIST PIG. Are you ready to die?" After shooting the policewoman, Ben had fired a shot into Karpov's arm, rendering the old man helpless. His men - five of them - had to carry the Russian inside. Ben bound him to a chair in his basement apartment and switched on the lights, in order for Gregor to see his fate.

Gregor looked down at his feet. Ben circled him like a vulture. "You know, I shot your woman and that brat of yours just over there..." Ben pointed to the couch. Gregor sniffled. "And you haven't been doing drug deals, have you?" Gregor looked at Ben, surprise mounted in his eyes. "I found your...um...files? You were running an Addicts Anonymous or whatthefuckever down here, weren't you?"

Gregor nodded.

"So it's true!" Ben squealed with delight. "You *were* a Good Samaritan, even after your wife and kid got murdered by none other than yours truly. It takes a lot for a man to *not* want revenge."

Lindsey's body was stashed in the bathtub. Gregor could see her vacant eyes staring back at him. He knew he was about to die, and in a way Gregor welcomed death. He had helped hundreds of young drug addicts sort out their lives and no one had ever asked him about his alleged "drug ring". It was never a meth lab - Gregor had worked tirelessly across the years to save as many people as he could. It was atonement, Gregor's burden to carry. He'd paid the price for being selfish, so an unselfish life in the service of others was the only way he could live. He was ready to meet his wife and daughter again; it was time. Gregor knew it. He just prayed that Mia would be the survivor of Samuel Murray's cruel *War Game*.

Ben ripped off the duct tape from Gregor's mouth. "Any last words?" Ben asked.

"*Bozhe, ya proshu vas, chtoby ukhazhivat' za Mia. Da svyatitsya imya Tvoye...*"

"The fuck? Russian? Oh well..."

Ben pulled the trigger. A bullet swept through Gregor's brain and the old Russian died with a smile on his face. Tears streaked his cheeks. Happy tears.

Forgiven tears.

God, I beg of you to look after Mia. Hallowed be thy name...

CHAPTER ELEVEN
8:30PM

Nina handed out Mrs. Rose's assortment of cookies. Brad, Kenny, Mia and Gloria each wolfed down a couple with a glass of milk.

Nina wanted the scene to appear normal for Mia's sake. She couldn't risk losing herself to terror. They had all heard the gunshots and the screaming that emanated from the ground floor, as well as the first floor. The gunmen were moving quicker and more efficiently than Nina had wanted them to move, they would arrive on the fifth floor in no time.

Nina wished the small pistol didn't dig into her back so. Nina wished many things, like gunmen dying, Mia surviving...she thought back to her childhood. She had been so happy and content with life back then. Where did it all go wrong? When she fell pregnant with Mia? When she had unprotected sex with Vincent? When was the moment Nina's life changed forever?

"You okay, my dear?" Kenny asked. Nina blinked twice. She'd zoned out again.

"Yeah. I guess."

"Listen..." He took Nina's elbow and steered her away from the group. "I didn't want to say this in front of that lovely daughter of yours, but we have to do something. We can't just sit around waiting to be picked off. Let's fight back."

His tone was urgent.

"How? I have a small pistol and a bad temper. How are we ever going to eliminate these people? They're brandishing fucking assault rifles!"

"Keep your voice down, Nina." Kenny was paternal, but in a charming way; Nina found it patronizing. In fact, Nina found most men patronizing. Daddy issues. Or a problem with God - Nina never understood her rebellion against the male species.

"What's the plan?" Nina asked him.

"Guess what was my job before I became a -"

"Don't tell me, you're a porn director..." Nina smirked.

"Let me finish. Before I got involved with the 'porn industry'" - air quotes - "I lived a lie as a straight man."

"Many gay men do that." Nina cocked her head to the side.

"Yes, well, I was one of them. I was also an NYPD detective."

Nina gasped. "Are you shitting me?"

"Why is it so hard to believe?"

"No. No, I mean, I never pictured you as an ex-cop..."

"What did you picture me as, then?"

"Uhm...an interior designer?" Nina laughed. Kenny wasn't impressed.

"You do know that gay stereotype is bullshit, right?"

"Sorry..." Nina blushed.

"Anyways, long story short, I worked on a case in this building."

"What kind of case?" Nina asked, tentatively. Kenny rubbed his fingers together. "I guess you know about what happened in your apartment?"

Nina nodded.

"Well, I was the lead detective on that case. The Merkovitz family."

"Maria was one of my best friends..." Nina muttered.

"Is that so? Well, the murder was unique. No one had a clue how twenty gunmen could enter a building and murder an entire family without anyone saying anything."

"This is the Murray building you're talking about. I'm still waiting for *The Shining* twins to pitch up at the elevator."

Kenny laughed.

"The Merkovitz case drove me insane. I was suspended from the force..."

"Why?"

"I couldn't let go...and I *may* have entered Samuel Murray's home without a search warrant."

"*The* Samuel Murray?" Nina eyed Kenny suspiciously.

"Yes. I broke into his home. God...the things I found...you know he was a modern day Nazi? That's why he murdered the Merkovitz family."

"It never went to court?"

"Lack of evidence." Kenny shrugged.

"Jesus," Nina said it too loudly. Mia scoffed at her mother. "Sorry, sweetheart!"

"So why move into the building?"

Kenny considered his answer for a moment.

"To tell you the truth..." He sighed. "I don't know. I guess I wanted to be closer to the thing that had driven me insane."

"I was walking amongst the fires of Hell, delighted with the enjoyments of Genius; which to Angels look like torment and insanity," Nina said stoically.

"What?"

"William Blake. The poet?"

"Ah, yes." Kenny smiled. A peculiar warmth and empathy bled from his eyes. Nina found him irresistible; she liked men who *understood*. Not just understand, but really *get it*. And Kenny - damn him for being gay - had that within him.

"So who is Brad? Your boyfriend? I mean, the kid's a bit young -"

Kenny burst out laughing.

"Nina...my dear! Brad is my porn boyfriend."

"Your...what?"

"We shoot movies together and upload it. We're not *together together*. I have been single for as long as I can remember."

"Why? Haven't you met the right guy yet?" Nina asked, immediately taken back by her own brashness.

"I am a bit difficult. I get bored easily. My ex-wife - yes, I had a wife once - bored me to death with her endless stories about Tupperware, the Republican Party and, get this, she once took me to her church so I could watch an 'exorcism'."

Nina laughed so loudly that she snorted. Twice. Brad gave them both a foul look.

"God. Are you serious?"

"Yes! The demonically possessed girl writhed on stage while she uttered orgasmic and sexual platitudes."

Kenny took Nina's hand. He held it, his fingers stroking her knuckles softly. She didn't wince or pull away.

"I have another secret..." Kenny's eyes twinkled with delight.

"And that is?" Nina asked.

He pulled away from her, sighed and said, "I have three 9mms in my safe. I kept them from my detective days. Never handed them in. Lied...told them they got stolen. Now if we can get those guns..."

Nina shook her head. "No, Kenny. It's too risky."

"I'll sneak out, slip downstairs, get the guns and come right back. I promise, Nina; I have to try."

Brad interrupted them. "I know you two are busy swooning like a love-struck couple in a *Mills and Boon* novel, but if we don't get ourselves to a safe place...well, no more cookies for us."

"Brad. Kenny suggested that he goes down and gets the 9mms in your safe. There's three -"

"Not a fucking chance!" Brad yelled.

"I am going, Brad. Alone!" Kenny scolded him.

"Brad, I don't like it either...but we need firepower..." Nina looked at her feet as she spoke; she didn't want to meet Brad's screaming white stare.

"It's settled, then." Kenny smiled *that* smile again, and Nina's insides tumbled around like a boat caught in a hurricane.

After a round of hugs from everyone, Kenny kissed Brad on the cheek and slipped out into the hallway. The overhead lights were dimmed. Kenny struggled to adjust his eyes to the low light. He had to move briskly, the gunshots had ebbed away earlier, but he knew they could just as easily start up again. A bizarre, tight-skin silence slicked through the air like a chill wind.

Kenny shivered. He opened the stairwell door and crept down the steps. *One at a time. Don't make too much noise...*

After what felt like an hour, Kenny finally reached the second floor. He slid open the door to the staircase and sprinted down the hallway. He fumbled with the keys, missing the keyhole twice. "Christ..." he muttered.

Click.

He was inside.

The safe sat safely tucked away behind the bedroom cupboard. He'd had the foresight to install a small lamp above the safe - just enough to illuminate the area which housed the thing - no one could see it from outside. Kenny pulled the string. The light clicked on. Now he just had the combination to deal with; *19 97 11 22.*

Beep!

He grabbed the three 9mms, a wad of cash (one always needs cash) and a report about the Merkovitz murder. Kenny pushed everything into his gym bag.

The bag slung over his shoulder, he rapidly headed for the door, the exit, the stairwell, Nina, Brad. His heart pumped manically.

Blood rushed into Kenny's ears, a tinny sound reverberated through his body. *Low blood pressure.* Upon reaching the staircase, Kenny heard several gunshots come from downstairs. He had to move! In a half-hunched motion, Kenny sped up the stairs and pushed open the door to the fifth floor.

He had one final hurdle - the hallway which led to Mrs. Rose's apartment. Without thinking, Kenny ducked and ran. His shoes pounded the carpet, his eyes longed for the door handle; his movements, although lithe, were slightly unsteady.

Kenny tripped.

He hit the floor, hard - something snapped, something bled - but Kenny scrabbled to his feet and kept going without a moment's hesitation; if the gunmen found him in the hallway, they'd have shot him on sight.

Thankfully, *mercifully*, Kenny reached the apartment before anyone saw him, and flung open the door. Nina threw her arms around him in a sisterly embrace. Brad cried. Gloria mumbled, and Mia chewed on a plastic Dora the Explorer water bottle.

Thus, the bizarre family of circumstance came together. Reunited, they had hope.

They had guns.

CHAPTER TWELVE
9PM

The girl's red fingernails *click-clacked* as they moved swiftly over the keyboard. She typed in the bank account number and wired several million dollars to an offshore account at the push of a button.

She lit a cigarette, leaned back in the chair and admired her handiwork. Five hundred million dollars had just been sent to seventeen different bank accounts across the world. Samuel Murray's entire estate now lay in the hands of greedy bankers at every corner of the earth. No one could have traced the money - Maddy Murray made sure of that.

She'd met Samuel while she worked on a cruise liner as a waitress. And, at the tender age of nineteen, Maddy had inadvertently caught the eye of one of the wealthiest men on the planet. They married six months later.

Now, at the age of 21, Maddy had enjoyed the unorthodox pleasure of administering Samuel with a lethal dose of Propofol. He'd wanted to die on his own terms, and who was Maddy to get in the way of a sick old man and his death?

She was also well-versed on the subject of the *War Game*. Maddy had singlehandedly activated the process exactly 24 hours after Samuel gave out his final breath.

Unbeknownst to everyone in the building, Samuel had the genius forethought to install hidden cameras during a 'building inspection' last March. And so, Maddy could see every tenant, every gunman, and every gruesome death in crisp, clear, high-definition.

The footage was being streamed out live via the Dark Web, and pundits placed bets on who they thought would survive the *War Game*. Mia, the five-year-old Italian girl, was in first place. People couldn't imagine a world where a child got murdered for $100 million, no one was that cynical, not even Maddy.

Oh, if they knew my plans...

Maddy wanted to be part of the action; a mischievous bystander with a hidden agenda. She wanted mayhem and bloodshed and horror and murder and fuck, what else? What else, except for more money than God, could Maddy Murray possibly want?

Simple; she was thirsty for revenge.

Once that was out of her system, Maddy planned to go global with the *War Game*, perhaps even selling the rights to the highest bidder. A different building. More structured. Less baggage. More money. Maddy had a business plan that most evil geniuses would have killed for, and she knew it.

Her lazy blonde hair curved around her swimmer's shoulders and slept at her back as she walked through the enormous rooms in Samuel's mansion, Maddy's burn-brown eyes stark reminders of a life of love without reciprocation. Dressed in a black miniskirt by *Dolce & Gabbana*, Maddy looked evey bit the part of the mourning widow; she even wore a sequined veil for extra effect.

Snap snap.

Maddy clicked her fingers. Flora, the housekeeper, came in with a tray. Maddy grabbed it from her and set it down on the desk. A beautiful bottle of the greenest Absinthe stood in the middle like a forgotten centerpiece.

"Come, Flora! Let's drink!" Maddy proclaimed loudly.

Flora suffered a smile and nodded. Maddy poured them each a glass of the strongest alcoholic beverage this side of Amsterdam. Flora sipped, while Maddy gulped it down.

"Is nice, isn't it?" Maddy motioned for Flora to finish her drink.

Flora, the elderly Hispanic housekeeper had been looking after the Murray family since the early 70s. Although Samuel was a hardened anti-Semite, he had been inexplicably drawn to Flora; Maddy had never understood the attraction between a Jew hater and his Hispanic housekeeper.

They weren't intimately involved - ever. Flora had been more like Samuel's confidante and best friend; he trusted the woman with his life. Maddy had adored Flora the moment she met her, a happy, rotund woman with a shaded complexion and heavy eyes. She had escaped to the United States after losing her family to a drug lord in Mexico, a feeling Maddy knew all too well - which was perhaps why Maddy felt such a kinship with Flora.

"Flora, what's your salary again? Sorry, but Samuel never told me."

"Please don't fire me, Mrs. Murray...I can't survive without my job."

"I would *never* fire you!" Maddy gave Flora a warm hug.

"Then why you ask my money?"

Mandy sighed. "Just tell me, Flora. Trust me on this." She put her hand over the housekeeper's. It was rough around the edges - Flora's past showed up loud and clear in her calloused palms.

"One thousand dollars per week," she finally told Maddy.

"Let's do something about that, shall we?" Maddy opened the desk drawer and pulled out a checkbook. She scribbled down a name and several numbers, ripped out the check and handed it to Flora. The Spanish blood that rummaged through Flora's flesh rose to the surface of her skin. She fell to one knee. "*Dios mios...*Mrs. Murray...I can't -"

"Go, live your life, Flora. You'll be okay. Come here." Maddy embraced the old woman like she was her own mother before she cast a parting glance at the slightly crumpled check in Flora's damp hands:

$5 million US DOLLARS
MS FLORA HERNANDEZ
SIGNED - MADDY MURRAY

NINA SEEMED FRANTIC. Frayed. Agitated. She paced around Gloria's apartment like a tortured weasel. Kenny, Brad and Nina all had a 9mm, while Gloria kept the small pistol she had given to Nina earlier. They were armed, but they still had no plan.

"So, let me get this right. Only *one* of us can walk out that front door tomorrow morning?" Brad asked. The nervousness made his voice tremble.

"Yes," Nina said. "Except if we somehow beat the game...break the rules, you know?"

"And how would we do that?" Brad's voice was edging closer to hysterics.

"We play the game, I guess?" Nina shrugged. Mia was sitting on her lap. Her pacing annoyed the child, so Nina sat down when she'd finished her fiftieth round. The air around them felt languid, like an oil spill on a summer's day.

"Why haven't we heard more gunshots?" Kenny asked. He was playing poker with Gloria. Each sucked on a cigarette.

"Maybe they gave up?" Brad had hope - endearing, yet naive. Dangerous.

"No..." Nina muttered. "I think they're preparing for the final showdown. Are your weapons loaded?"

Everyone nodded in unison. Jumpy Brad circled the table where Kenny and Gloria were seated. Nina watched the young, amateur porn star pacing the room like she had done moments earlier. Something was off. Nina couldn't quite put her finger on it. Something in Brad's bursting blue eyes flickered like a final realization. It was as if he had finally given into his fear. Or wanted more; adrenaline is a dangerous drug.

While Nina soothed Mia by brushing her hair, Brad moved to the kitchen. He was a few feet away from Gloria; he stared at the old woman as if she had all the answers.

"Yes?" Gloria put down her cards and looked directly at Brad.

"You're old."

"So?" Gloria stubbed out her cigarette.

"We still have lives to live. I mean..."

Kenny smashed his fist into the table.

"What the *fuck* do you mean, Bradley?" Full name; that was anger at its best.

"N-n-nothing. I just thought, you know?"

"No I don't know, Bradley. Why don't you enlighten me?" Kenny, clearly agitated, stood up and took a hurried stride towards Brad. The young man cowered.

"I-I-I just thought that if it comes down to it, shouldn't the youngest person survive?"

"That's Mia. Not you." Kenny prodded Brad's chest with his finger. He was about to launch a punch at Brad's face - Nina sensed it. She felt Kenny's agitation and fear mixing into the menagerie of madness that surrounded them.

"Fuck off, Kenny." Brad was resolute, Mia covered her ears.

"Hey! Stop swearing in front of the little girl!" Gloria demanded.

"I don't give a fuck anymore, you old bat!" Brad screamed. His voice went hoarse.

"What did you just call me?" Gloria asked without blinking.

"Yeah! That's right. You're an old bat who is going to die soon. Why should we keep you alive? Huh?" Brad reached for his 9mm, but Kenny punched him before he could grab it. Brad went down heavy, like a sucker punched boxer. He clutched his jaw and stared furiously up at Kenny and Gloria. Nina settled Mia down and walked over to where Brad lay slumped against the kitchen counter.

"Hysteria won't save us," Nina muttered.

"Neither will you, you teenage mom whore!"

Oh no, he didn't.

"Brad, what did you just call me? A whore? This coming from a porn star? Listen, dude, I think you'd better just fuck off, right now." Nina straddled him. She used her backhand to slap him hard across the face. Brad's head hit the side of the counter and lolled to the left and Kenny and Gloria were suddenly very afraid of Nina's temper.

She looked at them. "What?" she asked.

"You just knocked him out cold," Gloria whispered. Her hand to her open mouth.

"Why did you do that?" Kenny asked her.

"He called me a whore. And he would have shot one of us eventually."

"Violence is the final resort. We're supposed to be civilized! Better than *them*!" Gloria pointed at the door.

"Sorry. I just don't like wise asses."

Nina walked back to Mia, picked up her little girl and went to the bedroom. Kenny and Gloria sat in stunned silence. Brad groaned, Kenny rushed to his side.

"You don't call Italian women whores, Bradley. What were you thinking?" Kenny said.

"Fuck you, you old, perverted faggot!" Brad got up, pushed Kenny out of the way and stormed towards the door.

"Open that door, and you die." Gloria said calmly, her pistol held gracefully, aimed directly at Brad's head. Nina touched Gloria's shoulder gently. "Put down the gun, Gloria. Brad won't leave. He knows better." Nina's voice dipped low.

"The fuck? You can't tell me what to do," Brad growled.

"Yes, we can, Bradley." Kenny's voice was much calmer, but it also carried a dark, sinister edge.

"You're all insane! I'm leaving!" Brad opened the door.

A flash of light escaped Gloria's pistol. Nina and Kenny recoiled, shocked, as Brad's head exploded into a hundred pieces; brains and eyes and slivers of shattered skull landed in the hallway. The amateur porn star slid lifelessly down the door, marking it with a gruesome rouge.

Kenny shrieked. Nina gasped.

Gloria smiled. The old woman had tasted blood now, and she wanted more. Before Nina could cover her body, Gloria fired two shots into Nina's left arm. Kenny flinched when a third bullet grazed his knee.

Bloody tears streaked down Nina's arm. Although the pistol Gloria had was small in comparison to a 9mm, it still packed a deadly punch. Mia appeared at her mother's side, the poor child an inconsolable mess.

Gloria pouted and fired another round - the bullet embedding itself in the living room wall.

Nina screeched like a banshee. Gloria, sweet old Gloria, had not only succeeded in murdering Brad in cold blood, but she'd also fired shots at her, Kenny, and worst of all, young Mia. If that last bullet hadn't strayed and smashed into the wall, Mia would have surely been dead.

God Himself entered Nina's adrenaline-fueled body - she zoomed in on Gloria's face like a missile, pulled an unseen trigger from her unseen gun, and fired as many shots as the weapon allowed.

The slugs ripped through Gloria's old body, tore through her breasts, slamming into her chest, forcing her heart to explode.

Rivulets of dark, crimson blood streamed from every orifice in Gloria's body. It gushed from her nose, lips, neck, knees...red arcs exited her throat, spraying the apartment with every last drop of blood Gloria had left in her dying body. The woman went down on her knees, flipped backwards and slouched down in a bizarre sitting position - she looked like some weird Yogi-turned-serial-killer.

Even Gloria's hands had been ripped apart by Nina's bullets - several fingers missing, and one knuckle carved to the bone. Nina had never seen anything remotely close to what Gloria had become when she'd unceremoniously pulled the trigger on Kenny's 9mm.

She didn't know how she'd mustered the anger to do it, but still, *she* had killed the sweetest woman she'd ever met. Gloria had like a mother to her, but she had been forced to protect Mia. Gloria was bound to have killed Mia as well, wasn't she? *Wasn't she?*

Nina didn't see the blackness envelop her vision - she was still screaming when she dropped into a violent vial of unconsciousness.

CHAPTER THIRTEEN
9:30PM

Maddy arrived at the Murray building in a limousine. She noticed the cop car she'd seen on the feed - it looked less imposing than it did on her screen.

The building itself towered above Maddy like a gargantuan obelisk, or some magnificent church on the outskirts of Dante's Inferno. It held both hope and pain, sorrow and happiness, gore and beauty, life and death; brazen contrasts that tickled Maddy's spine as she exited the vehicle.

She thanked Tim, the driver, and told him to head home. Still dressed in her little black number, Maddy had something else on her body - a sheath on her back. Inside, hidden from view, slept a weapon more powerful even than Ben Sussman's assault rifle.

Maddy had begun her training with the weapon the moment she'd been able to form ideas and walk. She was just three years old when Magai Nyasaka had adopted her and taken her to Japan to raise as his own -even though Maddy had less Asian genes than a warm-blooded American from Kansas.

When he passed away, Maddy - still only sixteen years old - packed her clothes in a bag and returned to the US. Her adoptive father had taught her well - her daily lessons with him had included The Suppression of Revenge; mock battles in the courtyard and a two-hour history lesson on Kamikaze behavior. Maddy had been filled to the brim with deadly knowledge, had read Tolstoy at the age of seven and could write entire essays in Japanese, French, Italian, English and German by the time she'd turned ten. In short, Maddy was a child prodigy, a genius with an IQ of 160, and a calm, humbled, modern woman; the quintessential amalgam of childhood-trauma-turned-positive mixed with a wisdom older than Jesus.

Maddy held her smile until she reached the entrance. "Gregor Karpov...you did well, my old friend," She whispered. She removed a small remote from her handbag. Red, blue and black buttons stared back at Maddy like evil, wanton eyes. The red button meant instant death, whilst blue led to a complete shutdown of the electrics inside the building, and black opened every single door. Maddy duly pressed the black button. The steel door that covered the entrance whirred to life. Slowly, lazily, the door raised itself into the confines of its protective lair.

Maddy gasped when she saw the horrific scene before her, Ben Sussman sitting on a pile of bodies. He smiled at her with red stained teeth.

"Jesus..." Maddy whispered. And closed her eyes.

MIA WAS SOBBING. KENNY had pushed the child into the bedroom and shut the door; he didn't want her wide, innocent eyes to witness more death. She'd seen enough. She'd just witnessed her mother unloading an entire clip on Mrs. Rose, the dear old lady who gave out those cookies, milk and Dora the Explorer cupcakes. Kenny soothed the little girl, rubbing her head, he pulled her close against his chest.

"Don't worry. Don't worry. Everything is okay," Kenny whispered. If only he could believe it himself, Kenny knew nothing was going to be okay, and the chances of him surviving this were slim to none. And strangely, Kenny was at peace with these thoughts; he'd willingly sacrifice himself for the lives of the young woman and her child. He knew he really had little choice, so Kenny planned his suicide - go to his apartment, lie on the bed, play some Neil Young and pull the trigger. Nothing special about it, Kenny thought.

Just a quick, painless departure.

Nina burst through the door. Her manic, intense eyes searching the room for Mia. Her left arm was bandaged - Kenny had administering to her wounds. The bullets had ripped through the soft tissues of her arm, so she hadn't been in any serious danger. The bleeding had stopped when Kenny poured dusty white peroxide on the wounds, and Nina passed out. Twice. The wounds had fizzled for several minutes while Kenny held Nina's head with his hands and pinned her legs with his, despite the fact that he thought he'd been shot near the knee; it turned out the bullet had merely grazed his skin as it ripped through his jeans. They'd then moved Gloria and Brad's bodies into the living room. Kenny covered them with white sheets that quickly turned a dark shade of crimson.

"Is Mia okay?" Nina asked, breathlessly.

"She's okay. Shocked, but okay. How are you holding up?" Kenny's empathic eyes bore into Nina's soul, her panic lifting in an instant.

"Well, the adrenaline wore off. My arm hurts like a bitch, but I'll be okay. I can't believe I did that..." Her voice hitched and trailed off.

"Listen," Kenny said, before steering Nina to the bed where she slumped into a crying heap. "You saved our lives, Nina. Goddamit. I'm sorry it happened, I really am so sorry, but you saved us. You saved Mia. Sometimes we do things to protect those we love. *We have to.* Survival of the fittest."

"Why did she start shooting?" Nina asked, her eyes blushed with sadness.

"I guess her survival instincts kicked in? Maybe she just wanted it all to end? We'll never know what her intentions were. But I can assure you, Nina, Gloria Rose wanted to kill us."

"Really? How sure are you?" Nina asked. Kenny pointed to his leg and Nina's arm.

"Proof?" he asked.

"I know she shot *at* us, but what if -"

Kenny touched Nina's shoulder. He wrapped his hand around her clavicle and soothed the tense muscle there.

"Stop thinking about 'what if'. You did what you had to do. You saved two lives - mine and Mia's."

Mia had fallen asleep on the bed. Nina looked at her daughter and her tears dropped on Nina's hands. The fear and the horror and the bullets and Kenny and Mia and everything that had ever happened to Nina came rushing back into her consciousness at once, it was overwhelming.

She allowed Kenny to console her. Nina crept into Gloria's bed and allowed herself to rest beside her daughter.

"Rest now..." Kenny whispered. And he felt his own eyes close.

BEN SAT ATOP A PILE of severed legs and arms, and spilled brains and blood. He had single-handedly murdered each and every one of his fellow mercenaries —he'd even bitten off Jeremy's ear in his murderous frenzy.

Something had snapped inside of Ben's already fragile brain, something so insidious that not even he could wrap his head around it. He giggled when he saw Maddy, she glowed in the light, her skin the color of almonds that had roasted in the sun, her stunning eyes sharp and crisp and lit up from within.

"Benjamin? What the fuck have you done?" Maddy stared at the pile of bodies that surrounded the mercenary. She couldn't believe it, Ben clearly didn't feel guilty about his actions.

"I killed them all," Ben whispered.

"This is a mess. People are paying good money to watch the War Game. Do you even realize how many viewers we might have lost?" Maddy didn't really care - she just wanted Ben to feel bad.

"Mrs. Murray, why are you here?" Ben asked without looking up.

"To play the game."

"Pardon me?" Ben stood up, and slipped twice on the blood drenched floor.

"You don't think the master is allowed to play the game?" She crossed her arms.

"You have Mr. Murray's money -"

"Oh, I'm not doing this for money. No, Benjamin. I've been waiting *such* a long time for this." She grinned.

Ben felt uneasy. Ben never felt uneasy.

"You've been waiting for this? You're just a kid..."

"Am I, now? You see, Benjamin, I have the power to ruin your shitty little, rich-ass existence. I now have unbridled power."

Ben took a hold of his assault rifle. Just in case.

"You'll be dead before you come close to my real life. Bitch," Ben spat.

Maddy laughed. "Is that how you talk to your wife when you're fucking her?"

"You leave my family out of this, you gold digging cunt!" Ben pointed the assault rifle at Maddy.

A woman's voice suddenly made the room feel pregnant with reality, "What in God's name..."

Ben looked at the entrance. There, beneath the fluorescent harshness stood none other than Susan Sussman, Ben's wife.

She vomited against the wall, her eyes wide and arresting.

Black hair shadowed Susan's lean, tanned shoulders. She was clad in a cocktail dress - the emerald green one Ben had bought her for their anniversary.

She was a strong woman, a force to be reckoned with in court, and stronger than Maddy thought. When she'd sent the text - *meet me at the Murray building: surprise!* – Maddy had doubted that she'd show. It was late, and she couldn't possibly leave the kids at home, but she had; *Anything for her husband,* Maddy thought.

Ben crawled to his wife. His burnt face bathed in massacre and blood, his hands pressing into brains and mutilated body parts.

Squelch.

Squelch.

The sound of horror hungered after Maddy's bile, which rose in her throat. She gnashed her teeth and managed to keep the sickening tornado in her guts at bay.

Susan was so horrified by the scene before her, that she kicked off her high heels and rushed barefoot to the door. Maddy pressed a button on the remote. The doors clicked shut. Susan shrieked.

"Susan, baby! I can explain," Ben pleaded.

Susan spun around and gave Ben a murderous stare. "Get away from me! You monster!" she yelled, and. Maddy laughed.

"Benjamin, I don't think your wife loves you anymore," Maddy said.

"Fuck you!" Ben screamed at Maddy, his voice hoarse and broken.

Susan's entire body heaved with sobs. She fell to her knees and Maddy felt a pang of sympathy for the woman; finding out that one's husband is a murderous monster can be awfully rough on the psyche.

"Please, let her go. She has nothing to do with this!" Tears traipsed around Ben's pink face. He was begging. *Good.*

"Now, why would I do that?" Maddy asked him.

"She's innocent!" Ben cried. "Please, Maddy! Please!"

"Susan?" Maddy turned her back on Ben - a dangerous, yet calculated move. Susan looked at Maddy with contempt and fear in her eyes.

"Y-y-yes?" a tremble in her voice.

"Should I let you go?" Maddy smirked.

"Please...I won't tell anyone. I'm a lawyer. I am sworn to secrecy."

Maddy reached into the sheath at her back. She felt the cool handle, the contours and curves of the weapon. She pulled - the blade slid out with a whistling whine. It flashed in the light like a gunshot. Susan's eyes bulged. Ben whimpered.

"What I have here was given to me when I turned nine. I've been training with it ever since. This, my dear friends, is one of the oldest Samurai swords in history."

An entrancing weapon indeed, a sword that whistled as it swept through the air. The hilt had intricate designs carved out by centuries of work, the image of a viper curled around the front or the blade, etched into the steel like an ancient tattoo. Maddy held the sword with both hands and kissed the blade before turning around once more. Ben's hand was on the trigger of his assault rifle.

"Are you going to shoot me?" Maddy asked.

"Yes. Susan? Honey? Run. Just run, okay?"

Susan leapt to her feet and ran down the hallway. Maddy watched her disappear into the darkness of the lift. Not a sound. Just the light pit-pat of her bare feet on the carpet.

And then the blade came down on Ben's right arm.

CHAPTER FOURTEEN
10PM

Ross and Tamara Whiting lived on the fourth floor, he was a construction worker, she a nurse. The couple had moved in when their son Jason was born.

Jason turned sixteen two days before the Whiting family boarded up their apartment to keep the crazed gunmen at bay. Ross and Tamara were on sick leave, as both of them had caught a nasty flu the previous week. And, Jason skipped school because he didn't study for an AP CHEM test - he just pretended to be sick. The Whiting family rued the fact that they were all home when the shooting started.

"If only I'd gone to work," Tamara lamented and Ross told her that at least they were together as a family – and what if they had come home and got shot before they reached their apartment? Jason would have been orphaned.

Tamara agreed with her husband, but still chastised herself for not taking precautionary measures. She knew how dangerous the area was - why didn't they move to New Jersey when they'd wanted to? They had enough money. Ross would have been out of a job, but Tamara knew her husband would have quickly bounced back. Although they were the only African-American family in the building, none of them ever felt ostracized. After all, the Murray building celebrated diversity, despite the rumors that Samuel Murray was a racist and anti-Semite.

Tamara was a petite, lean woman with wild hair and emphathetic eyes - a stark contrast to Ross, who was a boulder of a man with a gruff, authoritative voice. Jason had inherited his dad's height, but his facial features were an exact replica of his mom's; warm, welcoming, gentile.

Ross and Jason were barricading the door while Tamara poured herself a calming drink in the kitchen. As Jason hammered the final nail into the barricade, a burning-white shriek filled the hallway. Jason looked to his father. Tamara dropped her glass in the kitchen.

"Anyone! Please! Oh God, help me!" None of the Whitings had ever heard such a terrified female voice; she sounded like she was being burnt alive. Or butchered.

"Dad, we have to help her!" Jason began pulling the barricade apart. His father stopped him with a slap to the head. Jason, shocked and in disbelief, had never been hit by his father before. He stared at the man who he'd thought would never harm him. Tears sprang into his eyes. Tamara saw the violent outburst, but did nothing, she knew the risks of opening the door and allowing in a screaming woman. Knowing Jason, Tamara also understood that her son was like her - altruistic with a bleeding heart.

"I'm sorry, son. I really am, but we have to consider our own safety first." Ross reached out to touch Jason, but his son flinched, stormed away and slammed his bedroom door. Ross caught Tamara's stare. She smiled gently.

"I don't know what came over me," Ross whispered. Tamara touched his arm. "You did the right thing. Tough love, maybe?" She was a graceful, caring wife, and Ross loved her more than life itself. And he loved his son so much that he sometimes ached on the inside.

The screaming woman banged on the door, the entire apartment rattling as if caught in an earthquake. Tamara bit her lip. Ross noticed a tear on his wife's chin, but neither made a sound; they merely stood at the door, flinching each time the woman brought down a fist.

"My name is Susan Sussman. I'm a lawyer. If you let me in, I can pay you! Please!"

Tamara spoke softly, "I am sorry, but we can't risk it." Ross nudged her to keep quiet, but she shrugged him off and continued, "I'm a nurse. My name is Tamara Whiting."

Susan stopped banging. Tamara heard a squeak and knew that Susan had slid down the door, defeated.

"Do you have any kids, Tamara?" Susan asked stoically.

Tamara leaned forward, effectively closing the physical gap between her and Susan.

"A son. Jason."

Ross threw his hands in the air. He mouthed *What?* at his wife. Tamara nodded.

"I have two boys. Carl and Brent." Susan released a loud sob.

"You don't live here, do you, Susan?" Tamara asked.

"No. We live in the Upper West Side."

"We?"

"My husband and I. My family, I mean." Susan's voice was heavy.

"How did you end up here, then?" Tamara asked.

"Someone texted me, pretended to be my husband. I get here, and what do I find? The man I've loved for 22 years sitting atop a pile of corpses, drenched in blood and carrying an assault rifle. When I tried to leave, a girl - you won't believe this - a girl with a fucking Samurai sword locked me inside. My husband told me to run, so I did. I don't know what's going on." Susan sighed.

"We don't either. We just heard gunfire and saw a group of maniacs gunning down tenants in the parking lot. None of our phones are working - we can't even access the Internet."

"I think my husband was the leader..."

Tamara's body went cold. Ross shook his head vigorously, motioning to his wife that she needed to stop entertaining the woman.

"The leader of?"

"The head honcho. The main man. Looks like he murdered his colleagues, though."

Tamara's mouth fell open.

"They're all dead?"

"I think so. There's only the girl with the Samurai sword and my husband downstairs now."

"Are we safe, Susan?" Tamara asked whilst saying a silent prayer.

"No, because here comes the crazy girl with the sword."

DR. KAHN LIT ONE OF his Cuban cigars. He wasn't a smoker by any means - he only lit up on special occasions, and tonight was a celebration of epic proportions. Bathed in the dark gloom of his sparsely furnished apartment, Kahn took in the musky smell of old furniture and sighed.

His memories were filled with the depraved scent of formaldehyde; fifteen women had ended up in Kahn's 'practice' over the years. He usually removed their ovaries first, and then the eyes, the breasts, the lungs...he carved them up well. Organ harvesting was a lucrative business indeed.

Until a week ago, that is, when the FBI busted him and found human organs stashed all over his house.

If it weren't for Maddy Murray's quick actions, Kahn would have surely ended up rotting in prison forever. She'd informed him of an experiment at the Murray building, and although she didn't go into details at the time, the promise of freedom and $10 million had aroused Kahn's bloodlust enough for him to go along with whatever Maddy had in store. He opened the envelope he received from Maddy and read the letter for the fiftieth time:

Dr. Mehmout Kahn

My name is Maddy Murray, the soon-to-be late wife of Samuel Murray. I know all about your 'business'. The FBI will be raiding your house within the next 24 hours. I have included a key to an apartment in this envelope. Pack your things, and move to the address enclosed immediately.

I require your murderous expertise. I promise you freedom and $10 million if you do exactly what I ask of you.

The gunshots will initiate the experiment. Stay in your apartment. I shall knock on your door four times to announce my presence. Do NOT open the door for me. Instead, take the vial you used on your victims and leave your apartment.

I need you to eliminate everyone with a single injection of Propofol. Move slowly, deliberately. Stay in the shadows, and only stalk the living.

I know how you kidnapped those women - do the same for me.

Your future is beautiful.

Sincerely,

Maddy Murray

Dr. Kahn crumpled up the letter and leaned back into his chair. Two vials of Propofol lay on the kitchen counter. He managed to grab an extra vial for backup when he'd fled his home.

He glanced at the LED clock on the wall - 10:15PM. He'd wait for Maddy, even if it took all night; Kahn was definitely not going to prison. No, he had a more beautiful place in mind - South Africa, to be exact. He had family in Durban who always begged him to come visit. *I'd stay there forever,* he thought. He'd slip quietly into South Africa and live there for the rest of his life.

He'd could up shop again, be a *real* doctor for once. No more organ harvesting. Just the ocean and South Africa's sunsets as the backdrop to a brand new life. Maybe he'd finally get married. One of his victims was a blonde whore from Cape Town, she smelled like the wild night. He wanted a woman like that, a strong, South African bitch who'd do his bidding. He wasn't keen on slapping women around, but if they didn't listen...well, a couple of furious punches would be perfect.

Knock.

Knock.

Knock.

Knock.

Kahn muttered under his breath, "It's time." He waited several minutes before making his way to the kitchen.

Beneath the light, Kahn's face was illuminated. His dark-skinned lips were smoothed out by Botox; his eyes were carnivorous entities that could pierce the most cynical of souls; his distinctive nose – crooked, yet attractive – dominated his profile like a brush stroke. He picked up the two vials, inserted them into syringes and headed for the door.

He paused.

This was it. No more backing out. He would murder as many people as possible, and then some. Men like Dr. Kahn weren't built to be altruistic slaves to the machine - no, they were bred with the sole purpose to kill. A slight smile spread across his delicate lips. His gloved fingers curled around the handle, and he opened the door.

SUSAN'S RUN-IN WITH the sword girl was a short-lived affair. After she sliced Susan's shoulder, Susan punched the girl in the stomach and fled down the hallway. She climbed the stairs, stopping every ten steps to not only catch her breath, but to listen for any movement.

This was a hunt, and Susan was the prey. Susan arrived on the fifth floor. The hallway was the same as all the others - green, luminous carpet with emergency lights bathing the apartment doors in blue light. She couldn't look, so she turned and ran into a corner, her bleeding shoulder bumping against a latch. Susan grabbed the latch and pulled. Lo and behold, and much to Susan's delight, the door swing open to reveal a wooden, creaky staircase that led to a hidden attic of some kind.

It smelled like damp clothes and old smoke, but without thinking twice, Susan slammed the latched door behind her and climbed the steps. The darkness was so overwhelming that it reminded Susan of stories she'd read about sensory deprivation, where people were apt to go insane due to lack of stimuli.

As she neared the top, a light bulb lit up like a lighthouse in the distance. Susan fell on her knees and crawled towards the light. She didn't know where she was, nor if the light at the end of the literal tunnel would lead to suffering and death; all she knew was that she had to hide.

A cough. Susan stopped, pricked up her ears.

A ragged voice spoke from the darkness, "Come. Come! Come inside."

Susan didn't think - she stumbled towards the light, bumping her feet and knees on unseen trash, until eventually, she arrived at a small apartment. A kitchen table. A lonely couch. An old television set. A hookah. And a man.

A grey-bearded burst of manliness enveloped Susan before she could scream. He pulled away and eyed her quizzically. His eyes were a deep, dark mahogany with a swirl of yellow. He smelled *old*.

Susan sobbed. The man took her by the arm and led her to the couch in the center of the apartment. He motioned for her to sit down, so she did, but not without first taking in her surroundings.

"My name is Mr. Muhk. This is my home. Who are you, if I may ask?" He took a seat on the couch. He never faced Susan outright, but his eyes lingered in the corners like a shy child.

"My name is Susan Sussman," she breathed the words.

"You remind me of my daughter, Susan." He took a long pull from his hookah pipe. "Want some?" Susan shook her head. "No, thank you."

"Who cut your arm, Susan?" he asked.

Susan stared at him. "You won't believe me..."

"I'm 74 years old, Susan. I've lived a long life. Trust me, nothing can shock me."

Susan opened up to the old man. She told him everything; about Ben's deception, about the crazed Samurai-wielding girl, about the bodies, the Whiting family. She also spilled every secret about her past. Somehow, in some bizarre way, Mr. Muhk made her open up in ways she'd never dared to before. And, after she finished talking, Mr. Muhk lowered the hookah pipe and sighed. Tufts of white hair lined his bald head.

"Gregor was right, it seems," he muttered.

"Gregor?" Susan was thirsty, but she didn't want to take a swig of whatever potential poison Mr. Mukh may be hiding in his cupboard.

"He is - or *was* - the caretaker of the Murray building. But they killed his family. Two shots - one for the girl, one for the wife."

"That's terrible..." Susan whispered.

"Yes, but not as terrible as what is going on right now. You see, Susan, when I heard the gunshots, I didn't want to believe it myself. I mean, Gregor hid me up here to look after the building when he held his meetings. I'm the monster in the cupboard, you know?" Mr. Mukh took Susan's hand in his. "You are now a participant, Susan."

"Of what?" Susan's voice carried an insidious clarity.

"The *War Game*."

"I don't understand -"

Mr. Mukh got up and went over to his bedroom. Susan remained on the couch, dizzy and flustered. The old man returned with a piece of paper. A letter, Susan soon surmised, a letter which explained the *War Game* down to its finest details.

"This is impossible!" Susan shrieked.

"It *is* possible, and it's started. We have until, lemme see..." Mr. Mukh looked at his pocket watch. "We have until 6AM to survive. But like the letter said, only one can survive, so I guess it'll be a fight to the death at the end."

Susan recoiled from Mr. Mukh's stare.

"Don't worry, dear, I won't be murdering anyone anytime soon. You're safe with me. Only Gregor - and now you - know of my existence." Mr. Mukh touched Susan's hand again, a reassuring mannerism which he had practiced all his life. Mr. Mukh had never murdered a living being in his entire existence on this planet; he was a Hindu. All life to him was sacred. Even the strange woman in his apartment.

"Can you hide me?" Susan blurted out.

"*That* I cannot do, my dear."

"Why not?" Susan sounded more desperate than she felt inside.

"I plan to end my own life soon. I daren't take part in this horrible game."

"No! You can't die!" Susan grabbed Mr. Mukh and embraced him. Her eyes glistened.

"My dear, I have no choice. I cannot murder. Therefore, I have to end it myself."

"But *that's* murder! Come with me, Mr. Mukh! Please!"

"Would you care for a cup of tea?" he asked. Mr. Mukh's peaceful, deliberate stare gave Susan the inner strength to exact revenge on not only her husband, but also the designer of the sick game, Samuel Murray himself. Yes, he was dead, but if Susan survived the night, she'd go straight to the District Attorney and tell him everything. She nodded. She needed something to replenish her strength.

Several minutes later, Susan and Mr. Mukh sipped delicious Indian tea from fine china teacups, Mr. Mukh's rattling due to his Parkinson's disease. Susan relished the smell and taste; Rosemary. It soothed her hoarse voice and curled up in her stomach like a small embryo.

Neither spoke a word; Susan didn't want to disturb the moment with ragged, nervous hysterics. She knew what she had to do, and that was to survive. To be the last person standing; even if it meant taking out her husband, Ben.

Mr. Mukh gave her a gun. He was going to use it on himself, but felt that Susan needed it more than he did. She resisted at first, but finally relented when Mr. Mukh planted a gentle, grandfatherly kiss on her cheek.

"You have fifteen bullets. Use them wisely, dear Susan."

Mr. Mukh bade Susan farewell. She left the attic apartment, content that she had metamorphosed into a different woman. Mr. Mukh's memory and the lives of her sons hung in the balance, and Susan was willing to do anything to survive.

Anything.

CHAPTER FIFTEEN
10:45PM

Nina awoke with a start. She gasped. Gloria's bedroom was dark; someone had switched off the lights. She felt around on the bed - nothing. Mia and Kenny weren't in the room with her. She winced when she leant on her arm, but brushed it off as *just pain*. She hurried to the bedroom door.

First, she listened for any movement - anything that might give away imminent danger. Secondly, she turned the knob so quietly and efficiently that a cat burglar would have been proud. And lastly, Nina stepped out into the living room as cautiously as she could manage.

The sweet, throbbing smell of death assaulted her senses. A single lamp shone in the corner, Both Brad and Gloria's corpses were still covered. She scanned the room - Kenny had fallen asleep on the kitchen counter, but Mia was nowhere in sight. Panic rose in Nina's gut. As her breath quickened, Nina felt tiny fingers tug at her shirt.

She looked down and saw her daughter's face. Mia smiled. Nina couldn't smile back - she was too afraid that the vision of her daughter was merely a hallucinatory response to stress.

"Mommy?" Mia whispered.

Nina scooped up her daughter and planted her on the kitchen counter. Kenny groaned.

"Baby! Mommy was so scared, I thought you were missing."

"Mommy, don't be scared. Uncle Kenny said that you're strong and nothing will happen to us with you around." Mia curled her hand around Nina's pinky and they both shed a single tear.

"We have to get out of here, honey. You know that, right?"

Mia nodded. Kenny lifted up his face from the counter. Drool was plastered all over the side of his face. "Oh good, you're awake," he mumbled.

"Where was Mia while you slept, Kenny?" Nina's voice was laden with the authoritative tone she only used when upset.

"I didn't even know I'd fallen asleep..."

"You didn't look after her! Damn you, Kenny!" Nina slammed a fist into the counter. Mia started crying.

"Mommy! Don't be so angry with Uncle Kenny! I can look after myself. I *am* five, you know?" Mia hugged her mother and Nina's anger subsided somewhat.

"Yes, honey, but five-year-old girls still need someone to look after them, you know?" Nina glared at a dazed Kenny.

"Why does it smell so bad in here, Mommy?" Mia wrinkled her nose. She must've seen the sheets that covered Gloria and Brad; was she even aware that they were dead?

"Kenny, why didn't you keep Mia in the room? You know she saw...*that!*" Nina pointed to the sheets.

"Look, Nina, I'm sorry. I didn't -"

"We have to get out of here," Nina barked.

"The gunshots have subsided...but where will we go?" Kenny asked.

"We can go to my apartment, board it up properly. I'll take a gun and head downstairs to see what's going on. You stay here with Mia."

Mia shook her head. "Mommy! You can't leave me!"

"Baby, I'm only going to be away for five minutes. Kenny here will look after you, won't he?" That stare again. Kenny shrunk into himself. Mia looked up at Kenny. "Uncle Kenny, will you make me some pancakes?"

"Y-yes, Mia. Anything you want."

Five minutes later, the trio was set. Nina had a 9mm stashed in the side of her jeans, Kenny had one between his trembling hands, and Mia held her Dora the Explorer cup like her life depended on it.

Nina explained the plan; they were to leave Gloria's apartment and head straight over to Nina's. Whilst Kenny led Mia inside, Nina would head to the stairwell. She instructed Kenny to board up the apartment door with everything he could find, even if it meant disassembling the furniture. Upon Nina's return, she would knock on the door five times, and Kenny had to leave enough room for Nina to enter the apartment without having to struggle through the barricade. It wasn't an exact science, but really Nina had no choice. The plan was the best she could come up with.

She counted to three.

They rushed the door, popped it open and ran down the hallway. Nina covered Kenny and Mia. She scanned left and right, but there was nothing out of the ordinary, nor were there any hidden gunmen skulking within the shadows. She ushered Kenny and her daughter inside her apartment. Nina made to leave, and told Kenny to keep Mia safe at all costs, even if his own life was in jeopardy.

Nina left her crying daughter behind and headed to the staircase. She moved efficiently, like they did on the army shows she used to watch. She was a soldier now, the game had turned her into one, and God as her witness, Nina wasn't going to be a victim.

She fled down the staircase. The gunshots had indeed subsided; dare she hope that it was all over? Or was it just game over for Nina? When she reached the third floor landing, she slipped on something sticky, and looking down, Nina saw blood. A small splatter, but blood nonetheless. As she reached for the door to the third floor, a voice called out from behind her.

"Don't move." It was a woman's voice.

Nina held her hands in the air and slowly retreated.

"I said, *don't fucking move!* Are you deaf?" The woman sounded resolute. Stern. Empowered. Nina froze. She mumbled, "We can do this together...please, don't shoot. I have a five-year-old daughter upstairs."

"Cry me a river!" the woman yelled. "You're one of them, aren't you? One of the killers."

"No, I'm not." Nina tried to turn around to face her assailant, but the butt of a pistol slammed into the side of her head. Flashes of bright light clouded Nina's vision.

"I said, don't move, and what do you do? You move."

"I'm sorry. My name is Nina Corletti. Who are you?" she asked.

"None of your business. You came to kill me, didn't you?" The woman cocked her gun.

"Please, I beg of you...I'm in this with you. We're victims -"

"Shut up! Just *shut the fuck up*!" the woman screamed.

Nina fell silent; she figured the woman would have shot her already if she'd intended to.

"May I speak?" Nina whispered.

"Speak."

"I can take you to a safe place. My apartment is on the fifth floor. My friend, he is currently boarding up the place. I can take you there."

"And kill me? Fuck you!" The woman sounded hysterical.

A door banged downstairs. The woman grabbed Nina by the hair and pulled her into the shadows. Nina felt the woman's hurried breath hot on her neck. Both women stood there in silence, waiting for some madman to come dashing up the staircase and start shooting.

Footsteps. Loud. One. Two. Three.

"Do you have a gun?" the woman whispered into Nina's ear.

"Yes..."

"Take it out."

Nina did as the woman demanded; the 9mm pistol was heavy and cool to the touch. The woman spun Nina around.

Before Nina stood a middle-aged, blonde beauty without shoes, wearing an emerald-green dress that was caked in drying blood. The woman's eyes swept around Nina's face, as if trying desperately to find some form of kinship.

The footsteps neared. Nina and the woman melted into each other. *Don't breathe. Don't even think of breathing.* Nina's thoughts raced as the woman put a hand around Nina's mouth to silence her, its palm clammy and damp like underwear left out in the rain for too long.

A man dressed in a leather jacket moved past them. His gloved hands riled up the last remaining nerve Nina had in her body, and a dizzy spell overtook her. The man stopped. He looked into the shadowy corner where Nina and the woman hid.

He moved.

Closer, each step, calculated.

Nina saw two clear vials in his one hand; they were attached to lumbar puncture needles. *Death,* Nina thought.

The man sniffed at the air like an eager bloodhound, and Nina's skin crawled. The woman beside her dug her hands into Nina's face as the dark-skinned man hesitated for a moment, turned and ascended the staircase.

Once he'd shut the door above them, Nina sighed. The woman released her grip and shoved Nina into the fluorescent hue of the stairwell.

"I've never seen him before," Nina whispered as the woman held a gun against Nina's temple. Nina found that she was more afraid of the man with the vials than the rich blonde woman who held her life in her hands.

"My name is Susan," the woman said, before she lowered the gun. "And I can't do it. I thought I could, but I can't." Susan sighed. Nina gave her a small hug, this was a woman rattled by fear, not murderous intent, Nina could feel it in her bones.

"How did you end up here, Susan?" Nina asked her. Susan replayed the entire story but left out Mr. Mukh, for fear of him being caught. Nina nodded and bit her lower lip as a sign of sympathy.

"You got the raw deal, Susan. I know you think it's kill or be killed. But why don't we hang back for a bit and figure out how we can beat this game without dying?" Nina held out a hand.

Susan shook it. "Deal. Sorry for almost killing you..."

"No hard feelings. I'd have done the same," Nina said with a slight smirk.

"So, what do we do now? There's a family stuck in an apartment. Should we rescue them?"

Nina shook her head. "Let's save ourselves first, okay?"

Susan nodded.

"So what's the plan, Nina?"

"Well, since we can't use our phones or get onto the Internet, I assume they're using some kind of jamming device. If we can locate that and unjam the signal, it'll give us time to call for help. You said your husband – Ben? You said that he's in charge?"

Susan nodded again.

"Let's go downstairs. I'll hang back. Will Ben tell you where it is?"

"He's lost his mind – but maybe."

"Are you okay with this?" Nina asked in a soothing whisper.

"We don't have a choice, do we?"

"Afraid not..." Nina mumbled.

BEN LAY ON THE RECEPTION desk. The dizziness had subsided, but the pain in his severed arm was worse than the burns he'd received during his time as a soldier. *At least the bitch closed the wound by burning my stump*, Ben thought.

After Maddy sliced off Ben's arm, she'd dragged him to Karpov's apartment, lit the stove and pressed the bleeding stump onto a stove plate. Ben had passed out almost immediately from the pain. He'd screamed, though, screamed until his vocal cords tore and bled into his mouth.

Ben knew he was going to die, so he went for a lie down on the reception desk just to recover from the pain. He must have fallen asleep, because when he opened his eyes, Susan stood before him. Her shoulder was sliced to pieces, and the dress she loved so much was caked in black blood crusts. She said something, but the buzzing in Ben's ears kept out the sound.

"I can't hear you!" Ben's voice was over-loud, like a klaxon going off. Susan mouthed the words once more, *Where is the signal jammer?*

"The *what*?" Ben shrieked.

Susan grabbed Jessie's notebook from the desk. A string connected a ballpoint pen to the inside. She wrote:

Where is the signal jammer? I need to phone the boys.

Ben shook his head. "Fuck you for asking, Susan! You know I can't tell you that."

Stop being a dick! Give me the location!

"I shall *not* compromise this mission."

Ben, if you don't give me the location, I'm going to shoot you in the kneecaps!

"Fuck you. Do it."

Susan pulled out her gun and fired two shots – one in each knee. Ben's kneecaps exploded with a pop, blood and bone fragments littering his body.

"Oh Jesus! Fuck!" Ben squirmed like a tormented lab rat. He reached out for his assault rifle, but Susan shot him in the elbow before he could pull the trigger. Ben didn't scream this time; he simply grunted and passed out again. Susan took the rifle off her unconscious husband, just as Nina appeared behind her.

"God...Susan..."

"The fucker had it coming," Susan whispered. She spat on her husband's twitching body.

"I know..." Nina had no words.

Susan checked the assault rifle. "How do I use this thing?" She laughed. Nina felt the urge to giggle, too – traumatic situations changed people, and weird reactions were apt to bubble up, like the urge to laugh when someone dies.

"We gotta wake him up, Susan."

"I know, but he isn't giving -"

A gasp rippled through the tight atmosphere. "Jesus Christ..." someone said from the shadows. Nina and Susan turned around, aiming their guns at the darkness. Nina's throat constricted with fear and Susan trembled.

"Drop your weapon, and come out with your hands raised!" The words left Nina's mouth before she'd even thought them. *Instinct.*

A timid, albeit strong African-American woman came out of the shadows. Hands raised above her head, she walked cautiously towards Nina and Susan. She was crying.

"My name is Tamara Whiting," she said. Susan immediately lowered her weapon. "Tamara? It's me. Susan."

"Susan Sussman. I remember."

Nina asked whether they knew each other, to which Susan replied, "Tamara gave me the strength I needed to get my ass in gear. They're the family I told you about. What are you doing down here, Tamara? It's not safe."

Tamara lowered her hands. "I needed to get out. My husband tried to stop me, but I pushed past him. He's still holed up there with my son." Tamara's eyes scanned the gruesome scene in the lobby. Blood, entrails, brains...everywhere.

Unable to help herself, she choked up and puked. "I've been an ER nurse for twenty years, but I've never seen anything like this. Jesus..."

How much do you know about what's going on?" Nina asked the woman, her voice masked with apprehension.

"About *what*?" Tamara looked at Nina like she was an alien.

"Good. Better that way."

Susan frowned. "Nina..."

"Tamara, the less you know, the better." Nina raised her gun again.

"Are you crazy?" Susan shrieked.

"We need to protect ourselves, remember?" Nina was cool, calm and callous.

"You can't just go around shooting people! Lower your damn gun, Nina!"

Tamara looked at the pair of bickering women with puzzlement. "I can go. You don't *have* to shoot me, you know?" she said.

Suddenly, as if she'd suddenly snapped awake, Nina registered what she was about to do. She lowered her gun.

"I'm sorry -"

Bang.

Bang.

Two bullets plowed through Nina's torso. Her body jerked. Once. Twice. And she collapsed.

A guttural, disembodied scream tore through the air as Tamara pounced on Nina's body and applied pressure to the exit wounds – one in her stomach, and one just below her left breast. A frothy red spilled from Nina's lips as she gasped desperately for air and tears streaked down her face.

Susan puked all over herself – again. Tamara was screaming something about her applying pressure to the wound, but Susan's mind had completely checked out and left the key at reception.

A trail of smoke curled away from Ben's assault rifle, and on his face was etched a mixture of agony and joy and lust and death.

Each time Tamara compressed the gaping hole in Nina's chest, a fresh river of blood cascaded down her neck. She was still moving, but agonizingly slow, and Susan watched as the woman's existence faded away before her very eyes.

Tamara, bloodied and sobbing, stopped and bowed her head as Nina's eyes turned one last time and settled on Susan.

Susan looked at Nina's vacant stare and nodded in acknowledgement.

PART TWO: RAISING THE STAKES

CHAPTER 1
8 HOURS UNTIL THE FINALE

Maddy Murray cleaned the blood off her sword. The blade had sliced through two drug addicts on the third floor – decapitation was always a bloody affair. Maddy stepped out of the gooey gloom that emanated from Karpov's basement apartment and applauded Susan, Tamara and Ben.

Clap.

Clap.

Clap.

"Well, well, well, the harrowed protagonist suffers a premature death; I couldn't have written this little narrative better if I tried! Congratulations, you guys!"

Maddy stepped over Nina's lifeless, bleeding body. She slid the sword back into its sheath. "Susan, I see you've survived? And *you*," she pointed at Tamara, "your name is Tamara, yeah?"

Tamara nodded.

"Oh, and lest I forget, Benji 'Bad Guy' Sussman! Who blew off your legs, Ben? Susan, your own darling wife? Tsk tsk."

Susan recoiled, burrowing herself in the corner behind the reception desk where Ben lay.

"Don't be so scared, Susan. Goodness. It's not as if I'm going to kill you anytime soon.'

Maddy brushed away a blonde lock that stuck to her blood splattered cheek. Tamara turned to run.

"Stop! Or Ross and Jason die."

Tamara's composure cracked. "Look, lady, I don't know what the hell is going on, nor do I care. I just want to get back to my husband and my son. That's all. I don't care if you slaughter the entire population of New York City." Tamara's nostrils flared as fear made way for anger.

Maddy cleared her throat. "Tamara, as much as I'd like to erase your memories, I simply can't. Like it or not, you are now a participant in Samuel Murray's *War Game*."

"The fuck?"

Maddy explained the rules of the deranged game to Tamara. The once petite, lean woman who'd worked as a nurse for so many years lost all sense of self as she discovered the deadly brevity of her situation. Mortified by the reality of it all, she fell to her knees and prayed, *"our Father, who art in heaven, hallowed be thy name..."*

"Shhhhh!" Maddy silenced the religious soliloquy. "For God's sake, stop your hysterics, Tamara. You might even win the game. Who knows? You'll have to kill your husband and son, but hey, immortality always comes at a price."

"Kill the bitch!" Ben spat out the words like a man possessed.

"Susan? Why don't you join your friend Tamara here for a second?" Maddy suggested.

Susan crept past Maddy, past her crazy husband, and worst of all, past the corpse of Nina Corletti.

"Great! You two make a fine team," Maddy giggled. "It's a pity Nina isn't still alive. Too bad I blocked her on Facebook...we were like sisters once."

Ben mumbled, "Huh?"

Even Susan and Tamara were surprised at this revelation.

"Oh, you don't know, do you?" Maddy smiled like some, sick, twisted child. "Back in 1997, long before terrorism and Twitter, a nice Jewish family moved into what eventually became Nina's apartment – the Merkovitz family. You *do* remember them, don't you, Ben?"

Ben mumbled incoherently; he was slowly dying.

"Of course, Ben remembers it like it was yesterday. I do too, I've been thinking about it for nineteen years. You see, I worked on the Merkovitz case," Susan said.

"Yes, you did. And did you prosecute anyone?

Susan lowered her eyes. "No...the leads evaporated. It was the one case I was never able to crack."

"And that's why you're here tonight!" Maddy slapped her palms together.

"*Marita Merkovitz...*" Susan gasped for air. The surprise made her head heavy.

"I changed my name to Maddy Wright when I turned sixteen; my plan was to stay hidden until I could exact my revenge. You know, I was only two years old when Ben ordered the execution of my entire family. The doctors said I couldn't possibly remember the event, that it was all nothing more than false memory. But I disagree; I remember my mother's face just before it exploded in a rain of blood, I remember the sheer terror in my father's voice the moment he knew that he was next. Do you know what his last words were?

Strach przed śmiercią wynika z lęku przed życiem. Człowiek, który żyje w pełni gotów jest umrzeć w każdej chwili," the Polish slipped from Maddy's mouth with graceful ease. "It means, '*The fear of death follows from the fear of life. A man who lives fully is prepared to die at any time.*' Mark Twain said it. Clever man he was, just like my father."

Susan took a few steps towards Maddy; she could sense the horrific pain in Maddy's voice.

"Don't take another step." Maddy pulled out her sword. It glinted in the light.

"Sorry, but I've been a nurse for twenty years. Maddy, or Marita, or whatthefuckever your name is, there's no way in hell that you would remember such a long quote. It's impossible! You're insane!" Tamara's anger spat out like a cobra's venom.

Maddy furrowed her brow. She pushed Susan out of the way and stormed at Tamara with her sword held high.

As Maddy reached her, Tamara ricocheted off the wall, losing her balance as she leapt away, and accidently smashed her forehead against the wall. Disoriented, Tamara fell, hands first, head lolling on her shoulder. She bit down hard on her tongue - the taste of blood filling her mouth. Tamara yelped like a kicked dog, which served to further aggravate Maddy's violent fury.

The sword came down in one fell swoop – and Tamara's severed right hand flipped over on the carpet as an bright arc of red sprouted from the wound. Tamara, unable to scream due to shock, used her remaining hand to apply pressure to the bleeding stump of her wrist. Blood gushed through her hand, spilling through her knuckles, and formed a ghastly pool of glistening maroon on the carpet. Maddy swiped the sword through the air again. Tamara didn't feel the blade curve into her left eyeball, nor did she see the clear goo leaking from her split eye; it was all too fast for her brain to register.

She lost consciousness soon after that.

A merciful reprieve.

DR. KAHN WAS DISAPPOINTED. He'd been stalking the building for what felt like an eternity, and not once had he found someone he could kill. That was, until he reached the fifth floor and heard playful banter between a child and a man. He stood by the apartment door and thought of his strategy – what to do? *Play victim? Be a policeman?* Dr. Kahn decided upon with the latter.

He knocked. The child's annoyingly squeaky voice fell silent. He heard footsteps.

A man's voice boomed from behind the door. "We can't help you. Please leave."

Dr. Kahn straightened his gloves.

"Sir, it's the police. You're safe. Open up so we can get you to safety."

"Which precinct?" the man asked.

"I'm part of the SWAT team. You've got quite a mess here, sir. We are here to help. Please let me in so I can safely usher you out of the building."

The man's voice wavered. "The SWAT team usually stays in formation. Why are you alone? What's your name?"

Fuck, Kahn thought. *He's on to me.*

"Brandon Lowell, sir. I'm still a rookie."

"Age?" The man behind the door wasn't going down without a fight. Thank God the peepholes were all sealed shut! *Voyeurism is fun.*

"Twenty-five, sir."

"Pardon my French, Agent Lowell, but you are sure as *fuck* not 25."

Kahn sighed. This was a tough crowd.

"Do you want the truth?" Kahn asked.

"Please. Enlighten me."

"I found out about the *War Game* online. I'm a medical doctor, you see? I had to do something to end it, so I snuck into the building and tried to rescue people. You're the first person I've spoken to who hasn't tried to kill me yet."

"So why lie?"

Kahn heard another set of footsteps approach the door. A little girl asked the man if it was her mother at the door, but the man didn't respond.

"Please let me help you and the child."

"I don't know…"

Kahn slipped his gloved hand into his pocket. He touched the vials. It aroused him. He always got hard while fingering the poisonous tubes. His unwanted erection pushed against his thigh; *no time for that!*

"You can keep a weapon trained on me. That way, I won't pose any kind of threat. I'd never harm you or your daughter, sir."

The bolts on the door creaked and groaned as it swung open. A wild-haired man pointed a 9mm at Kahn's head.

But, although the door was opened less than a sliver, Kahn had the know-how to disable a man with a door handle, stunning him in the process.

Before the man could register Kahn's gloved hands, a powerful kick slammed the door into his face. "Kenny!" Mia yelled out as the force broke Ken's nose and sent the gun spiraling away into the apartment. Dazed, Kenny stared at Kahn, unsure as to whether he should run or to hide.

Kahn's six-foot tall frame was an imposing sight –

it never failed to scare his victims witless, and he knew it; he'd always embraced his height, as it put him one-up on any potential kill.

"Mia! Run!" Kenny sputtered out just before Kahn smashed his face with a tight clenched fist. Mia stared at Kahn, unable to move, her tiny frame trembling with fright.

Kahn closed the door behind him and smiled. "Well, I've never killed a child before..." he whispered.

CHAPTER TWO
7 HOURS BEFORE THE FINALE

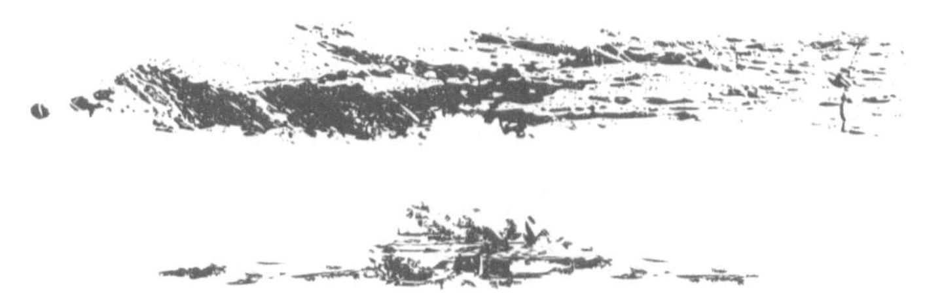

ROSS SHOOK JASON AWAKE, his son's sleepy eyes opening slower than a sloth's. "Jason, wake up." Ross's soothing voice masked the fear that danced in his eyes.

"What's going on?" Jason clambered out of the bed.

"It's your mother."

"What about her? Dad?"

Ross kept himself composed, even though he wanted to find Tamara and murder anyone in this nightmare who may have touched her. His rage was insidious and incessant, like a wildfire burning through desiccated old trees.

"She hasn't returned," Ross mumbled.

"Did she leave? Dad! What have you done?" Jason was beginning to sound hysterical.

"She wanted to go help -"

"We have to find her!" Jason yelled at his father, "when did she leave?"

"Jason, just calm down -"

"No! I *won't* calm down while Mom is still out there!" Jason slipped into a pair of jeans and pulled his head through a NYU hoodie he'd won in a poker game.

"You will *not* leave this apartment, you hear me, boy?" Ross couldn't contain his rage any longer, and Jason was to be at the receiving end – unfortunately.

"Dad, you know what? Fuck you." Jason punched his father hard in the stomach and ran to the barricaded door.

Ferociously, like a man possessed, Jason pulled the wooden structure apart within seconds and, before Ross could retaliate, he was out the door and tearing down the hallway.

Angry, panicked, Ross followed in his son's footsteps.

"WHY DID YOU DO THAT, *Marita?*" Susan, who had vomited again – twice, tried to reason with Maddy. If she could sway a jury, she could surely work her magic upon a vengeful 21-year-old.

"Stop calling me by my birth name!" Maddy shrieked at the woman.

Susan flinched, fearing the wrath of Maddy's sword.

Tamara lay unconscious in the hallway, and Susan couldn't stand the sight of her severed wrist and sliced open eye. She was still breathing, although each breath was shallow and raspy. Susan hoped that Tamara – the one who had given her strength earlier – would pull through, if only for her son, Jason.

An icy numbness had enveloped Susan's fragile psyche when Ben had finally died, just moments ago. She'd watched, sickened, as her husband of so many years was ritually disemboweled by Maddy. And Susan had lost her tenuous touch with reality when Maddy fed Ben his own intestines, which he'd gladly chewed like they were a piece of fine steak.

The crazed grin on Ben's face had sent Susan racing into psychotic territory – and she'd thought for a brief moment that the entire situation was a dream brought on by the anti-depressants she habitually took every night.

But the rank stench of Ben's disemboweling completely eliminated the dream hypothesis she had clung to since her arrival. This was all too *real* for a nightmare, too *visceral* – quite literally.

Susan tried again, "Why did you maim Tamara and murder my husband?"

"Because I had to." Maddy shuffled her feet like a naughty, chastised child.

"No, because you *wanted* to. You see the difference?" Susan hoped she could break through the seemingly impenetrable barrier of Maddy's villainous facade.

"So what if I like maiming and killing people? What's the problem?"

"You told me earlier about that Japanese man? The one who adopted you? Did he teach you how to kill? How to get revenge?" Susan's emotional capacity had greatly diminished following her husband's gruesome demise, and right now, she wanted nothing more than to escape the building with all of her limbs intact. And, with pressing Maddy's buttons that way, she was surprised that she still had all her limbs and that the insane girl hadn't come at her with that bloodied sword already.

It was a tricky tightrope – Susan knew there was no safety net; if she slipped now, she'd hit the ground hard enough for her organs to implode on impact. For her part, Maddy looked *into* Susan, as if she wanted to pull Susan's life force free from its hinges and spit on her corpse.

"Don't you dare lecture me on morality, *Susan*."

Susan stuttered, "N-n-no, I wasn't trying to lecture you. I just thought I could *help* you."

Maddy lowered her eyebrows. "Help me? Am I missing something here? How in all of *fuck* can you help me? You're just a widowed old cunt who thinks she still matters. Let me tell you, *Susan,* I would enjoy carving you up very much." Maddy hissed.

Susan suddenly understood everything; it didn't matter anymore, the *game* didn't matter, and nothing mattered except Maddy's personal quest to cross the Rubicon. Susan was merely a pawn in a terribly rigged system.

There was no war. In fact, Susan laughed at the thought, there was no game being played by unwilling contestants – this was all Maddy's own sick diorama; everyone else were merely actors she'd placed on death row. Poor, crazy Maddy was simply too lost in her own mind for Susan to reason with, she was a mere shell, hell-bent on killing and maiming everyone she came across, even if they'd played no part in the murder of her family.

And so, Susan resigned herself to the fact that she was *indeed* going to die that night, and that her children were going to be made orphans in one fell swoop. She wept at the thought of never seeing her boys again; loud, harsh sobbing that shook the Murray building to its core.

Yet, deep inside herself, where secrets hide, there lurked an inner strength Susan never knew she had, a strength so ferocious and powerful that slowly, surely began to consume her entire being.

After several minutes of crying, Susan realized she still had a gun tucked away behind the reception desk, she'd hidden it there when Maddy arrived. If only she could get to the gun, she was confident she could fire off a couple of shots at Maddy, perhaps even maim her, render her harmless. Susan couldn't kill the girl – what would happen if the *War Game* had no fail-safe and Maddy's death caused a premature end to everything? What if her death caused the explosives to go off? The building would be wiped away within seconds, and Susan, Tamara and the rest of the tenants would perish in an instant.

Maddy's back was turned – she was preoccupied with cleaning the blood and gore from her precious sword.

Now was the time for Susan to strike.

Crawling over pile of corpses, Susan made it to the bloodied reception desk. She scurried beneath and grabbed the gun, waiting for her where she'd left it. It was heavier than Susan imagined as she took the weapon into her trembling hands, stood up from behind the desk and aimed the weapon at Maddy's back.

Sweat dripped from Susan's nose and splashed on the blood soaked carpet. Almost preternaturally, Maddy knew what Susan was up to – she turned around with her sword held high, and stared directly into Susan's eyes.

"Drop the gun, Susan. Don't be a dumb bitch like your dead husband," Maddy snarled.

Susan shook her head, aimed the gun higher.

Maddy took a few tentative steps forwards, but Susan wasn't afraid of the Maddy/Marita hybrid, that fear had left her long ago. This was Susan the Attorney, the empowered female voice of reason, the prosecutor and the executioner.

"Not a fucking chance, Maddy," Susan whispered.

Maddy swapped the sword for a remote – a small, black thing with red, blue and black buttons protruding like angry zits. "Do you know what the red button does, Susan?"

"Let me guess, – it triggers the imaginary explosives?" Susan knew the explosives weren't imaginary, but she didn't want to trigger Maddy's violent mind.

Maddy barked a laugh. "Imaginary? Look behind you. Go on."

Gun still aimed at her nemesis, Susan took a step forward and turned towards the back exit. Sure as Satan's demise, a pack of plastic explosives was stuck to the hinges. A tiny, blinking red light was the only link to the remote, which could obliterate the Murray building in an instant.

Sweating, terrified, Susan turned around and gasped. Maddy was gone.

1988 - TOKYO, JAPAN

Magai Nyasaka sat at the very end of the mahogany boardroom table, his lawyers surrounding him like a mafia council.

The thin man opposite Magai was infamous for his underhanded dealings, his name was Samuel Murray, multi-billionaire and famously eccentric businessman.

Magai spoke fluent English; he'd studied at Oxford University for more than a decade, and with a PhD in Psychology, he understood the human mind far better than most; the psyche, the Jungian complexes, the Freudian slips. However, Magai had never met anyone as inherently vicious as Samuel Murray.

The American had made a multi-million dollar deal with Magai seven years ago, which had taken all of the Japanese man's savings. Everything he had. Samuel had promised that the money would go into a trust fund and double within a year.

But now, seven years later, Magai had learned that Samuel had lost the money in a bad investment – all of it, and Magai didn't have a single cent to his name. He'd sued Samuel for the money, obviously, but his own lawyers had advised him that his chances of recovering any of his lost money were slim to none. So, he called a meeting, invited his lawyers and Samuel, and was fully prepared to go to war for the chance to get any of his money back.

"Like I told you over the phone, Mr. Nyasaka, your money was lost in an investment. You knew the risks, hell, you even laughed when I told you that there was a miniscule chance that the money could be lost. Now you call a meeting? I had to fly seventeen hours for this?" Samuel's face blanched. He knocked the tips of his fingers together, his white-blue eyes staring straight ahead, entirely devoid of any feeling.

A slightly overweight lawyer spoke up in delicate English, "Mr. Murray, Mr. Nyasaka did not understand risk. He thought it safe."

"I'm sorry, but I can't understand your poor attempt at English. Magai? Couldn't you afford to hire a translator?"

"No," Magai spat, "you took all my money, Mr. Murray."

"Look, I can give you *some* of the money back. Would that put an end to end this pitiful charade?"

The other, more attractive, sharp-nosed lawyer shook his head. "No. Mr. Nyasaka wants *all* the money back. Not some. We go to court."

"How long have you been a lawyer, Mr...?"

"Kiratao. Mr. Kiratao," whispered Magai.

"Mr. Kiratao. You look like you still belong in law school. Are you sure you're qualified?" Samuel cackled like a witch.

Magai rose from his seat and approached Samuel, fists balled. He knew that if he was to punch the American, he'd never see a cent, but he was so enraged, this American's idiotic and racist approach that right now, fists seemed like the only option.

"Stop!" the overweight lawyer yelled in Japanese. Magai's nostrils flared. He punched the table hard and pressed his face against Samuel's.

"How much?" Magai asked.

"You mean money?" Samuel was great at playing coy. "Ten thousand dollars. Not a cent more."

Magai sneered, "Are you insane?! You owe me *ten million*!"

The lawyers shuffled about in their seats, uncomfortable with the sudden escalation in antagonism. Magai leaned over and grabbed Samuel's crisp, white shirt by the collar.

"You will pay for this, Samuel Murray. You will pay..."

Samuel smiled at the red faced Japanese man. "I guess not, Magai. I changed my mind; I'm not giving you a cent. Take me to court. I don't care. Now, if you'll excuse me, I have a flight to catch." Samuel stood up, nodded a cursory farewell at Magai and his lawyers, straightened his shirt and headed for the door. He paused. "They should have blown up every useless Jap when they dropped the bombs. Your kind just doesn't belong. Goodbye."

And at that moment, Magai Nyasaka formulated revenge in his mind, a plan so gruesome and horrific that it made his very soul crawl.

CHAPTER THREE - SIX HOURS BEFORE THE FINALE

Dr. Kahn eyed the man tied to the chair. He looked familiar. Kahn knew him, but couldn't quite place where they'd met. Kenny...?

"Were you a detective?" Kahn asked. Kenny nodded. "Oh my goodness, Detective Kenneth Bray, isn't it?" Kahn exclaimed. "You were the lead detective on the Merkovitz case? Oh, no – this is the apartment they were murdered in! You've got to be shitting me." Kahn laughed hysterically at his revelation.

Kenny looked at his feet. His hands were tied to the chair, and his feet were bound together with duct tape. He didn't know where Mia was, and all he could think about was he had to find her, protect her just as he'd promised.

But, Dr. Kahn had other plans.

"Detective Kenneth Bray – the cop who broke into Samuel Murray's house and held him at gunpoint for several hours. God, you were on every news channel in the country." Nonchalantly, Kahn reached over and stabbed Kenny in the leg with a butcher knife.

Kenny's scream was muffled by the panties Kahn stuck into his mouth. Nina's panties. *Where was Nina?* Kenny thought as he blinked away the unconsciousness that threatened him through the pain.

Kahn was growing quickly bored of torturing Kenny. He'd already stabbed the ex-cop in each leg, both arms, the butt, *and* sliced his Achilles tendons; now there was simply no more fun to be had.

Kahn had locked the kid in her bedroom and told her that if she screamed, he'd set the apartment on fire with her in it. The fear had silenced her, and Kahn hadn't checked her room in the two hours sincde. Why was she so quiet? Surely, she couldn't have fallen asleep?

Kahn opened Mia's door and was immediately assaulted by the smell of fresh air. Mia's curtains billowed inwards, bulging with each gust of wind.

The doctor scanned the room – in the cupboard, under the bed, behind the bed, in the other cupboard, behind the doll house, and there was nothing; Mia had disappeared.

Kahn's first instinct was to inject Kenny before chasing after the kid, but something – call it murderous instinct – told him to wait. And so he did, stock-still in the murky shadows of Mia's room, hardly breathing, barely moving a muscle. *Let the bitch come out,* Kahn thought. But time evaporated along with Kahn's patience – Mia simply was no longer in the room.

MIA'S FINGERNAILS DUG into the loose cement, her hair blossomed around her head with each gust of wind. It was a long way down, and she was sure that the fall would kill her instantly, and then she'd never see her mommy again.

While the bad man was hurting Uncle Kenny, Mia had slipped out of her window. She'd almost lost her balance during the initial descent but regained her footing on the foot-long ledge beneath her windowsill. She could see the police car below her; it was parked awkwardly, like in her drawings, before she'd learned how to color in properly.

Mia whispered the word *help* as loud as she dared, but the building was dead – *everyone* was dead. Mia felt terrified, especially when her bladder gave in to her fear and she wet herself. It smelled bad, and Mia didn't want the bad man to smell her.

She had listened to Uncle Kenny's screams as she'd escaped, and that had shaken her to the core. She told herself that none of this was real, but when the wind whipped at her thin frame out on that ledge, her stomach flopped and flipped. And, worst of all, Mia's tiny fingers trembled and ran slick with sweat, yet she had to hang on.

If she couldn't find, she had to survive.

Mia moved slightly to her left. Her foot slipped. She pulled her hands down to compensate for the sudden loss of balance, but it wasn't enough. Mia peeled away from from the side of the building and fell downwards, tumbling helplessly and up was down and down was up, she saw the moon and then the police car.

It was fast, faster than she'd expected, and as the ground raced towards Mia, she let out a silent prayer to a God she didn't know. Mommy had never taught Mia about God; perhaps if she had then she wouldn't be falling and she wouldn't die – because God would have rescued her before the bad man came.

Mia closed her eyes – people always did that when they braced for the inevitable – but the ground never came, Mia never hit the concrete.

As her nose brushed against the hood of the police car, Mia's body was violently jerked upwards and she felt her shoulder pop out of its socket.

Mia saw the building retreat into the distance.

Why was the building moving away? The invisible God she never knew tugged on a string and sent Mia spiraling back into the building. She smashed through a window, carved open her arm and fell face first into a vomit-colored couch.

Unbeknownst to recently orphaned Mia, thanks to fate or God or coincidence, when she'd slipped, her left foot had become entangled in the power line that ran the width of the building. The flex had wrapped around Mia's leg and served as a crude bungee rope and although electric sparks lit up the street like the Fourth of July, Mia landed safely inside an apartment on the second floor.

This odd moment of fate also gave the Murray building a much-needed reprieve – the power line sliced through the signal blockers at the side of the building, and severed power to the entire block. The hellish night, with all of its lights and lethal sparkles, died like a poisoned rat.

The darkness came to the Murray Building, and never left.

KENNY TRIED TO KEEP his eyes open. The power had gone out a moment before Dr. Kahn stabbed him in the shoulder, and now the room was black, so black that Kenny thought he'd gone blind.

He heard Kahn shuffling around, knocking things over, cursing and screaming. Kenny's phone vibrated in his pocket. It was an odd sensation, more so since there was no signal, so how was it possible? He squirmed in the chair, using his fingernails to cut through the binding that held his wrists. A fingernail popped off. Kenny embraced the pain, simply because it meant he was still alive. Another fingernail went. And another. Finally, Kenny's hands slipped free from the restraints. He pulled the panty out of his mouth, gagged and spat blood.

Kahn's heavy breathing was coming closer in the darkness; Kenny had to move, and quick. He loosened his feet, ripped off the duct tape and jumped out of the chair. However, Kenny's adrenaline forgot to warn him about the multiple stab wounds in his legs and arms. The pain, although excruciating, sent Kenny into a tailspin. He pitched forward and crashed against the glass coffee table, which shattered upon impact. Kenny knew Kahn was close – he heard footsteps near his ear.

Thump.

Thump.

Thump.

Kenny stopped breathing. He didn't move. Even though Kahn knew roughly whereabouts to find him, Kenny trusted that the darkness would keep him hidden until he could find a weapon of some sort. A soft, whirring sound rumbled through the building's interior. *Click, click, click.* The lights came back on. Nina's apartment was a picture of chaos – broken lampshades, torn curtains, smashed glasses; it looked like a crime scene, with Kenny as the victim.

Kahn was on Kenny before he could speak. He straddled him, pinning his arms down. Kenny struggled, fighting for just little more movement; but alas, Kenny wasn't strong enough to fight against Kahn's six-foot frame and the villainous strength that came with it.

"Stop moving!" Kahn yelled in Kenny's face.

"Let me go! Please, just let me go!" Kenny pleaded. Tears burst from his eyes, a bubble of mucous stuck to his nose.

"Shut the fuck up!" Kahn punched him in the face. Twice.

"Please..." Kenny mumbled.

Kahn dug into his pocket and wrapped his gloved fingers around the syringe filled with Propofol. He slipped the needle into Kenny's neck, depressed the plunger and watched as the clear fluid slipped into Kenny's bloodstream.

The disgraced detective squirmed as the poison entered his body. His eyes went wide, his lips turned blue. And then, Kenny, unable to breathe, unable to function, died without much fanfare.

Once Kenny's muscles went limp, Kahn stood up and brushed himself off. He eyed the fresh corpse lying amongst the glass shards. Kahn felt nothing. He didn't have a soul. He knew that, but he still wished that one day he could feel a pang of pity.

Kahn whispered, "God is dead, God remains dead, and we have killed him."

SUSAN WAS HIDING IN Karpov's basement apartment. Next to the bodies of Karpov and Officer Lindsey Moss, Susan had found a crawlspace where no one could find her. When the power went off, Susan had thought that the building was going to blow. And yet, not long into the darkness, Susan had felt the vibration of an emergency generator and the lights had come back on and blinded her.

The fluorescent bulb in Karpov's bathroom cast everything in a yellowish hue, which reminded Susan of child vomit, or the jaundice that accompanied liver cancer. Much to Susan's surprise, her iPhone had vibrated in her small clutch bag during the blackout, but after having eventually found the phone, Susan noticed that the signal was still nonexistent. She tapped on the *Messages* icon:

Mom, it's really late. Where are you and dad? I'm getting worried! Let me know, please. Love Carl.

Susan held the phone to her chest. Tears flowed from her like a waterfall; her teenage son was worried about her and Ben, his now dead father.

Susan's inner-survival instinct kicked in. She cocked the pistol Mr. Mukh gave her and slowly exited the crawlspace. Gun aimed at the door, Susan took a step, opened it and walked into Karpov's bare apartment where the television was tuned to static – *signals must have cut out when the power went off.*

Susan headed towards the hallway that led to the reception lobby. Someone was crying. Susan sought out the source – it was Tamara, stumbling around bodies, clutching her wrist *sans* hand, and trying to hold her sliced eyeball in its socket.

"Tamara!" Susan whispered loudly.

Tamara spun around. Her good eye saw Susan and bulged slightly.

Susan saw the dried tears that carved into Tamara's smooth skin, the limp wrist without the hand, and the rivulets of blood that streamed down her cheek to pool near her breasts. Tamara embraced Susan, both women close to hysterical. Susan held Tamara by the shoulders and said, "Listen to me; we're getting out of here. You and I. We'll survive this."

Tamara nodded. She didn't believe Susan, but there was nothing else to cling to. Even false hope took on a new meaning when you were fighting for your life. Susan grabbed hold of Tamara and stepped into the hallway which led to the rest of the building. She tripped over a rope and swore under her breath.

The rope made a resounding, *singing* sound and startled both women.

Tamara screamed.

Susan spun around to look and immediately regretted the decision. Tamara's husband, and son, were hanging from the rope; their intestines splashed across the carpet, bodies dancing at the end of the rope Susan had tripped over, their slack, dead faces marked with myriad cuts and burn marks.

Tamara ran to her son's body and pulled on his legs. More innards and bloodied gore tumbled out and bathed Tamara in a sickly rouge. The screams that came from Tamara tore through Susan's core and rattled her heart. Tamara, the once strong nurse, now lay sobbing amongst the entrails of her dead husband and son. She yelled at Susan, "Shoot me! Fucking kill me!"

Susan's body refused to move. She failed to realize that Tamara had already grabbed the gun and was pointing it at her own temple. Susan cried out, but Tamara pulled the trigger. A flash of brains and shattered shards of bone splashed against the wall; the entire rear of Tamara's skull was gone. She slumped forward, lifeless; her face smudged into the carpet and a wispy steam circling the back of her head.

Susan collapsed. She couldn't breathe. Her entire body seized up like a leg cramp and she curled into a fetal position and screamed and screamed and screamed until her throat bled.

Mercifully, Susan lost consciousness, and her sanity bled out of her, never to be regained. Susan, the strong, empowered fighter, lost her mind without knowing it.

CHAPTER FOUR - FIVE HOURS BEFORE THE FINALE

Detective Marita Merkovitz checked her digital watch again. Officer Moss had last checked in at 8PM, and numerous attempts to contact her failed. Captain Florez had phoned Marita and asked her to head out to the Murray building, that *something was seriously wrong.*

She hadn't been in the place since her parents were murdered in 1997, although sometimes she'd drive past it and try to remember what happened, how she survived, how she'd lived through the massacre; but it was as if someone had erased all of her memories.

She'd gone to live with her aunt in Ohio shortly after the massacre, and had dedicated her adult life to finding those who killed her family.

And she'd more than excelled; it was unheard of for a 21-year-old to become detective so quickly into her career. Marita, blessed with an IQ of 180, finished school at 14 and enrolled in the police academy at 16. By the time she turned 18, Marita had already advanced from Rookie to Lieutenant. Never before in the history of the New York Police Department had someone climbed the ranks so fast. They'd welcomed Marita into the force as if she'd always belonged there, her Colleagues referring to her as *The Genius Detective* and even made Dr. Doogie Howser jokes at her expense. Marita brushed it all off as nothing more than lively cop banter, but she knew deep down inside that she'd have to prove herself more than anyone else.

After becoming detective, Marita's incredibly analytical brain had deciphered clues left behind by a notorious serial killer that had been beyond her colleagues, and he'd been caught in the act of dismembering a woman. And so, Marita had been awarded a selection of medals, including one for courage and one for outstanding service.

They all knew that Marita was beyond her own intellect; not only did she have nerves of steel, but Marita could read a situation, analyze it and reach a conclusion within microseconds – it all made the woman one hell of a good cop.

Marita pulled up to the curb. The very sight of the Murray Building, which always looked so out of place – even at night – sent invisible spiders crawling down Marita's spine.

Lindsey's police cruiser was there, and parked at a strange angle. Marita got out of her car and headed towards the cruiser. Instinctively, Marita knew that Lindsey had been killed. She noticed the pockmarks in the police cruiser's interior, without a doubt impact marks left by an assault rifle's bullets.

The air reeked of gunfire and fear.

Marita took out her iPhone – she had to call the Captain to request back-up, because her own, new car wasn't outfitted with the standard NYPD radio gear yet. Marita stared at her phone. There was no signal. She held it in the air, turned around, walked back to her car, and repeated the process twice – nothing, not a single bar. To her knowledge, the Murray Building wasn't in some kind of cellular dead zone – people used their cell phones all the time to call the cops whenever hell broke loose in one of the apartments.

Marita espied a broken window on the second floor. She grabbed her gun and torch from the glove compartment. Switched on, the light from her industrial torch didn't even begin to breach the darkness in the apartment beyond the broken window.

"Scary, isn't it?"

Marita spun on her heels and shone the light towards the voice that came from behind her. An old Japanese man stood there, silently observing the building, and, Marita sensed, her.

"I am Detective Marita Merkovitz. Who the hell are you?" Marita lowered her gun. The torch still lit up the Japanese man's unkempt features. He was small, podgy, and his face carried years of worries.

"My name is Magai Nyasaka." The man's English was fluent.

"What is your business here? Why are you standing out in the street? It's dangerous, you know?"

"Oh, I know it's dangerous, Detective Merkovitz. I know all about the dangers hidden within the humble depths of the Murray Building. In fact, I know exactly what's going to happen to this terrible place come dawn."

Marita's Nordic features scrunched up. "Pardon? Did you just say –"

"Yes, I did, Marita."

"Detective Merkovitz."

"No, I think I'm going to call you Marita."

"Sir, please step back. Hands in the air!" Marita barked. She aimed her gun at Magai. He did as she commanded. "Now, get on the ground. Hands above your head! *Get down!*"

Magai dropped to his knees and crawled onto his stomach, hands locked above his head. Marita flipped out the cuffs she held in her back pocket. She wasn't going to arrest the old man – she merely intended to detain him. However, as Marita stepped off the curb and headed towards the old man, a sound echoed from behind her, one of keen steel singing as it sliced through the air.

Before Marita could react, Maddy's sword came down and slashed her neck. The detective stumbled, dropped to her knees, reached up to stop the blood from arcing out of her throat and collapsed, twitching violently upon the cold, hard ground.

Maddy, wide-eyed and drenched in human blood, stared at the detective. She thrust her legs into the air, tried to gain some breathable air, but the blood gushing from her throat brought her brain – and body – to a complete and utter standstill.

And so, Detective Marita Merkovitz, the real victim of the Merkovitz massacre, died at the hands of her doppelganger – a doppelganger who wasn't aware of her existence.

Maddy Murray believed from an early age that *she* was Marita Merkovitz, since her adoptive father told her so every single day. And then he'd died when she turned sixteen – or so she thought, because there, in the abandoned street in front of the Murray building, lay none other than Magai Nyasaka, the man Maddy had loved and adored.

He stood up from his concrete prison, broke the shackles of fear caught in Marita Merkovitz's eyes and said, "Hello, Maddy."

MIA AWOKE.

Her hand hurt from the glass that cut her. She moved her head, but a blinding headache and an odd sense of dizziness sent her back down into the couch. The apartment was dark, darker than her fears. It reeked of musk and rotten food. Mia gagged. What was going on?

Then she remembered the fall, her nose touching the police cruiser, how she'd swung back into the building and crashed through the glass. She also remembered how the bad man had tied Uncle Kenny to a chair and the way his lips moved when he told Mia that if she made a sound he'd burn down the building.

She's been locked in her room for two hours, weeping as she listened to Uncle Kenny's cries for help. Where was her mommy? Why was this happening to her?

A light!

Mia stumbled to the window and saw a blonde lady with a gun. Was she police? Could she help her? Mia called out, but her voice was too hoarse for the lady to hear. Something spooked the lady – it was a strange looking man. And then another woman appeared and killed the nice blonde lady with a sword. Mia had cried bitterly as she watched the scene unfold; if the police couldn't get to her, how was she going to get help and save her mommy and Uncle Kenny?

Never be afraid. Mommy used to say it to her when she was scared of the monsters that skulked in her closets. *Never be afraid of anything. You are strong, beautiful and wonderful. Never fear anything but fear itself.*

Another dizzy spell overtook Mia. She cried out for her mommy but knew in her heart that she was alone, at least for the time being. Then she heard footsteps. Mia was confused. Was it the bad man? Maybe it was Mommy? She had to get up, she had to escape. Mia forced herself to find the door to the apartment. She depressed the handle, but it didn't budge.

"Help me! I'm in here! Mommy?" she called out. Someone stopped at the door. She could hear breathing. It was Mommy, wasn't it? It could only be her! Not the bad man, not the lady with the sword. No, only Mommy.

A lady's voice responded, "Hello? Is there someone in there?"

"Yes! I am! Help me! The door won't open."

"Hold on, kid. Stand far away from the door. Quickly!"

Mia ran back to the couch and hid underneath it. At least it wasn't the bad man's voice.

Bang!

The door exploded in a rain of splinters and Mia tucked herself into a ball.

"Kid? Where are you?"

Mia didn't know if the lady was the bad lady with the sword from downstairs. Footsteps approached. Bare feet.

"Ouch! Fuck!" A shard of glass stuck to the lady's left foot. Blood poured out. "I'm not here to hurt you. Come out, please!" The lady ripped out the glass and stood on the balls of her feet.

Mia crawled out from beneath the couch. A blonde lady in a green dress stood before her, holding a gun. The lady's shoulder was sliced, and her nice dress was covered in what looked like blood. Mia whimpered.

The lady knelt. "What's your name, little one?"

"M-M-Mia Corletti. My mommy is Nina Corletti. We were with Mrs. Rose when people shot each other, and then I ended up with Uncle Kenny, but a bad man came and told me he'd burn me, and I fell and something pushed me into the building and –"

"Calm down..." The lady pulled Mia into her chest. It felt warm and welcoming, like when Mommy gave her a bear hug. "Mia, my name is Susan, okay? I'm not here to hurt you."

Mia looked up at Susan. Both had tears in their eyes.

"Why are you dirty?" Mia asked in a small voice.

"Oh, this?" Susan pointed to the dried blood. "This is only dirt. I was outside, and I tripped and fell in the dirt."

"Why do you have a gun?" Mia was relentless.

"So I can protect us," Susan sighed.

"From what?"

"From the bad people, Mia. Where is your mommy?"

"I don't know. She went downstairs and never came back."

Susan's eyes went wide. Realization hit her like an electric shock – Nina was Mia's mother. Nina who's corpse lay downstairs amongst all those ruined bodies; Mia was an orphan.

Susan's voice croaked, "Mia, I know you're young –how old are you?" Mia held up five fingers. "Okay, five! Well, Mia, you've survived a lot, why don't we leave here and go someplace real nice?"

"What about Mommy?" Mia asked.

Susan turned her head so that Mia couldn't see the fresh tears rolling down her already drenched cheeks.

"YOU'RE DEAD! YOU DIED! No!" Maddy curved the sword towards Magai. She was beyond hysterical – her face as white as ice, hands trembling, sword whistling through the air. "You're just a hallucination. That's all. You *can't* be real." Maddy closed her eyes, willing the apparition away, but a hand grasped her arm. She flicked it away, as one would a spider.

With Maddy's eyes still closed, Magai took the moment to enter the Murray building. He knew that once he set foot inside, he too would become part of Murray's sick *War Game*; it had been the plan all along and unfortunately, Maddy had to pay the price. She was Magai's way in, and she had to die because Magai had trained for years to win; he had no scruples about murdering the innocent girl he had raised.

"Stop right there!" Maddy shrieked.

Magai turned to face her. "Once I set foot in the building, I immediately become part of the *War Game*, do I not?" His tone was clinical, sterile.

"I swear to fucking God, I'll press the button and blow this fucking place to pieces!" Maddy's hands reached for the remote, her index finger lingering on the red button. She was just outside of the building, less than five feet away from the entrance where Magai was standing.

"Go on, press it," Magai whispered.

So, Maddy did.

She pressed the red button and waited for the blast wave to hit her, closing her eyes instinctively. One second passed. Two seconds. Ten seconds. She opened her eyes – the building was still standing.

Magai sneered at her.

"Why –"

"It doesn't work, Maddy."

"It does! How –"

Magai took the remote from her hand. She sensed her body moving inside and closing the door behind her. She had no control over her actions. *Was this shock?*

Magai crushed the remote with his boot. He picked up the pieces and handed them to Maddy. The remote, which Maddy thought controlled everything, was merely a piece of empty plastic. No wiring, no switches. It was a dud.

Maddy had risked her entire life – and the millions upon millions of dollars from Samuel's estate – for a plastic decoy. She tossed the pieces aside and righted her sword. The edge glinted near Magai's face.

"Who am I?" Maddy asked, the tone in her voice dead and buried. "Tell me, or I'll cut you in two. I don't give a fuck anymore."

"Your birth name is Bethany Anderson," Magai spoke with a calm resolve. "You just murdered the real Marita Merkovitz."

"No!" Maddy screamed furiously. "I am Marita Merkovitz!"

"No, Maddy, you're not," Magai whispered.

Maddy dropped the sword. She knelt – the breath punched out of her by Magai's revelation. If she'd paid attention, she would have seen Magai taking the Samurai sword into his own hands, she would have also have seen the blade slicing her head apart. But Maddy didn't, and her life flame was extinguished by her father, her mentor, her god. Maddy died with a question mark etched on her soul.

Bethany Anderson had been abducted from a nearby hospital when she was two years old. Witnesses described the man who'd snatched the child as *Asian*. They never found Bethany – she'd simply disappeared into the ether without a trace.

Now there were no more loose ends for Magai to worry about. His mission was simple – find every breathing person in the building, murder them, and walk away with $100 million at 6AM. He'd told Samuel Murray that he'd pay for what he did, but the eccentric old fool had never listened.

Maddy was never the fail-safe. No, it went much deeper than that. Magai was also marked for revenge by someone else, someone who had much closer ties to Samuel Murray than Maddy ever did.

And that person knew what to do when the time came.

The time when Magai Nyasaka decided to join the *War Game*.

PART III

REVENGE IS A DISH BEST SERVED ON A PLATTER OF HUMAN HEADS

CHAPTER ONE

Geneva, Switzerland - *PRESENT DAY*

Johann Weitzer placed his bet. He clicked on the name *Susan Sussman* and entered the amount: *$200 million.*

Five Ultra HD screens surrounded his desk. Each screen focused on a different part of the ugly old building – one aimed at the entrance, another one at the roof of the building. The third, fourth and fifth screens followed Susan Sussman and Mia Corletti as they traversed the third and fourth floors.

Johann's assistant, a peculiar-looking Dutch girl named Helena, wanted to know why he'd bet so much money on Susan – even she was following the *War Game.* In less than 24 hours, the competition had gone viral across the globe; at one point, three billion people tuned in to place their bets and watch the violence unfold.

It was, of course, illegal – akin to the proverbial snuff films, so every viewer knew how to vanquish any trace of them having participated. Weitzer Technologies, the biggest tech firm in Europe, secretly helped people to log on to its servers anonymously, and for every viewer that tuned in, Weitzer Technologies earned $100 US.

They were way past the $3 billion mark at midnight, Eastern Standard Time. And the money just kept on rolling in as more and more people clicked on the *War Game* website. And, Weitzer Technologies not only did a thorough job of erasing digital footprints, the company also warned journalists and whistleblowers that if they were to alert any higher authority, they would lose every cent they owned, and their digital footprint would include *child pornography, suicide assistance* and a *pledge of allegiance to ISIS* and was coded to trigger an alert at Interpol, the FBI, NSA, the CIA and every other international government agency.

Weitzer Technologies had become the biggest tech firm in Europe when CEO Johann Weitzer went into business with the NSA. Using a clandestine back door, Weitzer Technologies could tap into any person's digital life at the press of a button. They controlled the Internet, and they controlled access to the worldwide phenomenon of the *War Game*.

"Have you seen what she can do?" Johann asked Helena. "She's a *wunderkind!*"

Helena nodded. She didn't dare disagree with Johann. The six-foot, blond, blue-eyed Swiss national had been voted *Europe's Hottest Bachelor* in a recent online poll – he had it all, the looks, the personality, the business savvy, the ruthless streak that could stop someone dead in their tracks.

At only 25 years old, Johann inherited Weitzer Technologies from his father when he passed away in 2015. Johann was an only child, which made him the sole heir to the Weitzer fortune, as well as the only successor to his father's empire.

Johann reshaped the entire company – instead of continuing their focus on local banking security, Johann branched out and acquired an entire entertainment division, including the rights to the *War Game*. Maddy Murray had signed over creative control in the event of her death. And since she was killed by Magai Nyasaka a few moments earlier, Johann now owned every single aspect of the *War Game*.

Maddy thought she was going to survive, plus she didn't think clearly Johann told himself, although he didn't really care.

Helena didn't truly appreciate the *War Game*. She despised real-life depravity, but still couldn't look away, not when she'd just bet a year's salary on the little girl, Mia Corletti.

"Mr. Weitzer, do you want a cup of coffee, perhaps?"

Helena's Dutch accent irritated Johann. He shot back a curt, "Yes", without even looking at her.

Helena hurried off to make the boss's coffee when one of her colleagues, a gentle, elderly lady named Helga, stopped her for a bit of gossip.

"Helga, I actually have to go. I don't have the time, I'm sorry," Helena told the old woman.

"This will take a moment, yes? Just hear me out, okay?" Helga touched Helena's elbow, which was Helga's subtle way of reeling in victims to her gossip fest.

"What is it?" Helena asked, with irritation in her voice.

"Did you see that detective killed by Maddy Murray?"

"The *real* Marita Merkovitz. We know, Helga. Johann – pardon – Mr. Weitzer pulled the files immediately after it happened."

"Oh, but you don't know the half of it! Someone, who knows someone, told me that there is someone hidden in the building. On the disguised sixth floor!" Helga's excitement at this snippet merely aggravated Helena further.

"Impossible. We have the entire blueprint mapped out, showing us exactly where everyone is. We would have picked it up."

"Why did that Susan woman disappear after she joined the game?"

"There was a glitch. Tech fixed it. Now, please, I need to get coffee for Mr. Weitzer."

As Helena started walking, Helga popped up again.

"What if there's a secret contestant no one knows about? Shouldn't we tell Mr. Weitzer?"

Helena sighed.

"Helga, I can understand that this whole thing has taken you and the world by storm. However, if you go to Mr. Weitzer with this *false* theory, you're not only going to get fired, but you're also going to lose your bet. Come to think of it, how much did you bet?"

Helga smiled. "Everything I own. All my savings. Every cent. I'll earn it back."

"And whom did you bet on?"

"Susan Sussman of course! Okay then, let me get back to the game – and *work*." Helga chuckled.

Helena shook her head and hurried to the kitchen. *A secret contestant? Whatever, Helga,* Helena thought as she poured the coffee.

SUSAN AND MIA FOUND themselves on the fifth floor. The door to Mia and Nina's apartment was torn from the hinges.

"The bad man..." Mia whispered, almost inaudibly.

"Let's take a look. Stay behind me." Susan walked slowly, efficiently, gun held high. Susan turned the corner and entered the apartment, scanning every conceivable corner. No bad man, just a dead man. Susan pushed Mia outside. "Stay here, Mia, I'll be right back. Okay?"

"Yes, Susan." Mia nodded.

Susan went back inside. The apartment was in disarray; glass shards everywhere, broken lamps, torn cushions, blood. She checked Kenny's pulse, even though he appeared to be quite dead. He'd been stabbed multiple times, and Susan noticed a broken vial and a syringe beside him. She touched it. It smelled like poison – *how does poison smell?* Susan laughed at her own inexperience; she might have been a *tour de force* in court, but she didn't have the faintest clue how poison smelled. "Well, whatever it smells like, I guess it smells like this..." Susan muttered to herself.

Mia screamed. Susan cocked her pistol and ran to the door. There, a dark-skinned man with heavy and strange – yet not unattractive – features held Mia in a chokehold. A vial imbedded into a syringe poked out from his right hand, the needle was dangerously close to Mia's jugular.

"Drop the gun, or I inject this little cunt with a dose of Propofol. She'll be dead within seconds." He was tall, taller than Susan imagined the *bad man* to be. She duly complied and dropped her gun.

"Let the girl go. I'll take her place," Susan said without hesitation.

"Are you insane, bitch? I've been trying to find this little whore ever since she escaped. I knew she'd come back here. I didn't expect to see someone with her, though." He looked at Susan and a vile sneer formed on his lips.

"I dropped the gun. I did as you asked. Now let her go."

"Are you death?"

"Let the girl go, please. I'm a lawyer. My name is Susan, Susan Sussman. It doesn't have to be this way; you don't have to kill a child."

"The name's Dr. Kahn. Pleased to meet you, Susan Sussman." Kahn's voice tilted at the end, as if he was introducing himself in a purely professional capacity.

"Medical doctor?"

"Yes."

"So you took an oath – you can't take a life, Dr. Kahn."

"Who died and made you God?" The sneer was back; this man was pure evil, and Susan had dealt with serial killers before.

"Let me guess… you've killed before?" Susan crossed her arms.

"Yes. And I shall do so again."

"But you can make a difference, Dr. Kahn. You can let Mia go and leave this place. Whatever they have against you, we can take care of it. Now, please, I don't want to beg."

Mia started sobbing. Kahn pressed the needle into her skin but didn't pierce it. Susan flinched.

"You can't help me, Susan *fucking* Sussman. Neither can your courts. I have too much blood on my hands."

"I can help you walk free! I can do it, but you must give me a chance."

Dr. Kahn smiled. He had two options – kill the girl and the lawyer woman, get his $10 million and leave. Or he could take the lawyer woman's advice and let them go.

"Let me think for a second."

"We don't have time, Dr. Kahn. Please!"

"We have all the time in the world, Susan."

"You don't know, do you?" Susan asked.

"Know what?"

Within less than a minute, Susan explained to him the rules of the *War Game*. As she did so, his face went from anger to surprise, back to anger, and then to stoicism.

"No. It can't be."

"Yes, Dr. Kahn. You've been used by Maddy Murray."

And then it dawned on Susan – she shouldn't have told him that only one could survive, for now he had more than enough reason to kill them all. So she outright lied.

"Mia and I can't win – we were disqualified because we tried to attack Maddy Murray. But you *can* win! You're the only person left, as far as I can tell."

Kahn chuckled. He let go of Mia. "So I win?"

"You win, Dr. Kahn."

He dropped the vial of Propofol. Mia grabbed it and stuck the needle into his leg.

She depressed the plunger.

Surprised and aghast, Kahn stared at the deadly needle in his leg. Mia scurried away and joined Susan. Kahn mouthed the words *Fuck you* before succumbing to the lethal dosage of poison and stopped breathing within less than a heartbeat. His eyes rolled back into their sockets, a foamy froth expelled from his mouth as his limbs jerked once, twice, and that was it.

"Is the bad man...? Did I kill him?"

Susan grabbed Mia and held her close. What could she say to lessen the blow?

"Yes, but listen to me, Mia." Mia stared into Susan's eyes. "You didn't kill him, okay? He would have killed you. And me. You saved my life. You *have* to remember that and know that it's the truth, do you hear me?"

Mia nodded. Susan picked up her gun, held the child close to her body and headed for the latch which led to the secret sixth floor. If someone knew how to survive the final stretch, it was surely going to be Mr. Mukh, Susan knew that for a fact.

Her savior was above them, the proverbial God with the all-seeing and all-knowing eye – the man who had inadvertently saved Susan's life.

CHAPTER TWO
2:00AM

Magai Nyasaka struggled to breathe through the copper stink of blood that assaulted his senses.

Where was everyone? He found only bodies and brains and innards and fear and yellow goo against a wall. It was, quite literally, the massacre Magai had always dreamed of finding upon entering the *War Game*. He also knew there were still survivors roaming the building, otherwise the game would have already stopped with a God almighty explosion.

Magai felt uneasy amongst the dead. He'd hidden behind his own faked death for so long that he almost believed he was nothing more than a phantom circling the courtyard of life. His bones creaked when he walked, and his lifelong training with the sword was rusty at best.

Magai ascended the stairwell that led to each floor, stopping on the second floor to search every apartment. Only the dead surrounded him. Men, women and children, all shot to pieces by assault rifles; two freshly decapitated drug addicts – the list went on, *ad infinitum*. The third and fourth floor contained the same as the others – dead tenants and the sweet, lingering smell of death.

When he reached the fifth floor, something piqued Magai's senses. He found a dead man in the hallway, two oozing corpses covered with sheets in the one apartment, and another dead man without his fingernails nails in what used to be the Merkovitz apartment. Everywhere he went, Magai found insanity and the cessation of existence; nothing, not even his years of planning and training, had prepared him for this.

"Come out, come out wherever you are!" Magai yelled at one point, only to be met by the eerie silence. Frustrated, Magai headed to the stairwell – perhaps there were people hiding on the rooftop?

HELENA ERASMUS HAD been personally hired by Johann Weitzer. With no admin experience, Helena was thrust into a job where she had to endure late hours and the agonizing fear that her boss could, at his leisure, unleash one of his tirades at her.

She'd been called a whore, a slut, a worthless Dutch cunt, and her personal favorite, dumb bitch with small tits. Nonetheless, Helena endured the tyranny because the pay was excellent, plus she got to live in Switzerland, rent-free.

After the *War Game* became everyone's business, Helena had vowed to take a stand against her boss and leave the job with her head held high. Unfortunately, as with all major decisions in her life, Helena was simply too scared to quit. So, she joined in and played along when the violence erupted on the countless screens all across the building. She'd *ooh* and *aah* alongside her colleagues, mimicing their behavior, constantly afraid that Johann Weitzer would find out about her plan and murder her. Helena also had quite the imagination, which in turn, caused her to experience chronic paranoia.

During her lunch break, Helena drove to the outer edges of Weitzer Technologies, parking just a few feet shy of the boundary she wasn't allowed to cross during working hours. Helena's trembling fingers pulled out the iPhone she kept hidden in her car. She Googled the NYPD's number, her finger hovering over the dial button for several seconds – until she eventually gave in to her moral compass and dialed the number.

Ring

Ring

Ring

"You've reached the New York Police Department. To speak to an officer, please dial one. To speak to a detective, please dial two. Otherwise stay on the line – an operator will be with you shortly."

Helena bit her lower lip. She scanned her surroundings – she was alone. Not a security guard or, God forbid, Johann Weitzer himself, in sight.

"Welcome to the NYPD. Claire speaking, how may I assist you?" Helena was taken aback by the heavy accent. She cleared her throat and spoke.

"Hi, uhm, I need to speak to a – uhm, Captain Fernando Florez?"

"Pardon?"

"Captain Fernando Florez? Is he in?"

"Ma'am, it's two in the morning. The captain will be back at the precinct from eight AM onwards. You can call then –"

Helena interrupted the officer, "No. I can't. No. No. No!"

"Pardon? Ma'am, I need you to calm down. Are you currently experiencing an emergency?"

"Y-y-yes. I am, yes."

"What is the nature of your emergency?" the operator asked, lackadaisical.

"I can't tell you." Helena shivered.

"Ma'am, if you can't tell me, then I can't help you. If you refuse to give me information –"

"Terrorism!" Helena yelled the word louder than she wanted to.

"Excuse me? Did you just say *terrorism*?" The operator's voice was tinged with apprehension.

"Yes! Terrorism. In New York."

"Ma'am, giving out false information is a federal –"

"I need to speak to the captain!"

"Hold the line."

Click.

Helena waited for the line to connect. Several minutes passed by. She checked her watch – she still had thirty minutes before she needed to be back at the office.

"Deputy Lorrence speaking, how may I assist you?" A dark, heady voice. A *man's* voice.

"Sir, I need to speak to Captain Fernando Florez." Helena's voice withered.

"In connection with what, ma'am? You may speak to me."

"No, I have to speak to the captain!" Helena heard her hysterical voice rebounding on the international connection. She sounded uneasy and unhinged.

"Well, you're flat out of luck, lady. He won't be in before eight. Until then, you can either speak to me or hang up if this isn't an emergency. Your choice." Firm. Resolute.

Helena went with the former. She couldn't hang up, not after what she'd seen, not after that little girl was forced to kill the man in the hallway...

"My name is Helena Erasmus. I'm a Dutch national working for Weitzer Technologies in Geneva, Switzerland."

"And?" Deputy Lorrence obviously didn't have the patience required for his job.

"I am certain, no, I *know,* for a fact, that both Officer Lindsey Moss and Detective Marita Merkovitz are dead."

Deputy Lorrence coughed. "And how did you arrive at this conclusion, Helena?"

"I watched it happen."

"You *watched* it happen? And you did nothing?"

"The entire world did nothing, Deputy."

"I'm sorry, excuse my ignorance, but how in God's holy name does someone – who is currently in Geneva, Switzerland – know about the deaths of an officer and a detective of the NYPD? I have to remind you that lying to a law enforcement official is a federal, *international,* offense."

Helena's eyes blurred. Why was she crying?

"Deputy, if I told you the truth, I doubt you'd believe me."

Deputy Lorrence chuckled. "Try me."

"Do you know of the Murray building?"

"Yes. Everyone does. That place is creepy. You're starting to waste my time, Helena. Get to the point."

"My life is on the line here, Deputy Lorrence..."

"Okay, this has gone on for far too long. You're obviously be suffering from some kind of delusion or –"

Helena slammed her fist into the dashboard. She let out a tiny scream. "Listen to *me,* Deputy Lorrence! Send a team to the Murray building *now*!"

He laughed. "And why would I do that?"

"Are you near a computer?" Helena changed her strategy.

"Yes. Why?"

"Google Weitzer – that's W-E-I-T-Z-E-R – Technologies."

"Okay, I'm on their page."

"Click on the *WG* icon."

"Password protected." Deputy Lorrence sighed.

"Type in H-E-E-5-2-2-2-1. All uppercase."

Helena heard the *click-clack* of Deputy Lorrence's keyboard. She knew he'd find the truth as soon as he typed in her password. She checked her watch – ten minutes left.

The line went silent.

"Deputy Lorrence?" Helena looked at her phone. It was completely dead. "Fuck!" She banged her hands against the steering wheel. "No! No! No!" Helena burst into tears.

Someone knocked on her car window. She wiped away the tears and looked up, and there, standing next to her car in the open-air parking lot, was Johann Weitzer.

Helena clambered out of her car, spewed a bunch of apologies for being late and composed her trembling self. Johann merely looked at her, his face devoid of any emotion. *Did he know? Oh my God...*Helena thought.

"Helena, what were you doing in your car this far from the building?" Johann asked in that steely, terifying voice of his.

"Mr. Weitzer, I am sorry, I just needed some time to myself."

"Is that so, Helena?" Johann stared at the car, shifted his icy gaze to Helena and smiled.

"Yes, sir. I didn't want to, uhm, share my time – I mean my lunch break – with, uhm..." Helena's voice trailed off.

"Helena, I'm going to ask you a question, and how you respond will determine your future. Ready?"

Helena froze. He knew. She *knew* he knew.

"Did you phone the NYPD on a secret iPhone which you keep in your car?"

He is going to fire me...maybe even kill me. Helena's mind filled with a thousand possible scenarios, and none seemed to get her out of the situation she found herself in. Lie?

"N-n-never would I do such a thing, sir!"

Weitzer caught on, Helena saw it in his veneered smile."Helena, thank you for being an employee of Weitzer Technologies."

"Mr. Weitzer – please, I can explain. Don't fire me. Please!"

He laughed.

"Fire you? No, Helena, I would never do such a thing, especially not to an innocent little whore like yourself..."

Helena winced at his remarks, her tears flowing freely now, and without abate.

"So, everything is okay, sir?"

"No," Weitzer said in a low voice. "*Nothing* is okay. You just tipped off the NYPD and cost my company billions."

Helena dropped to her knees and begged her boss for forgiveness. "What are you going to do to me?" she asked.

"I'm not going to do anything. No, no, I might be ruthless, but I'll never hurt someone, especially a lady."

Helena exhaled for the final time, and one of Johann's black-clad bodyguards fired a bullet into Helena's left temple and she was dead before she hit the blacktop.

"Take care of it, will you?" Johann nodded to his bodyguard, turned around and walked slowly back to his building, whistling an off-kilter version of *Edelweiss*. Johann didn't get his hands dirty with anything so grubby as death – he paid people to do it for him.

Back in his office, Weitzer phoned the NYPD. He explained to one Deputy Lorrence that Helena was an ex-employee who suffered from a severe case of Schizophrenia.

And, although Lorrence questioned him about the *War Game*, Weitzer knew that the cop couldn't possibly have accessed the feed; while Helena had been busy giving out her password, Weitzer had changed it at the press of a button. Deputy Lorrence had been redirected to a webpage about eco-friendly products called *The War Game against Global Warming*.

And so, none the wiser, Deputy Lorrence accepted Johann's version of events and forgot all about the call from a hysterical Dutch girl he received at two AM in the morning.

"Madness is everywhere..." Deputy Lorrence muttered while he poured himself another cup of strong, New York coffee.

CHAPTER THREE
3:00AM

Mia and Susan sat silently in the yellow hue of Mr. Mukh's apartment. He offered them tea, which they graciously accepted. The attic, still as bare-boned and skeletal as Susan remembered, smelled like cheap incense and rosemary-scented tea.

Mr. Mukh sat opposite them in a large recliner, tugging at the tufts of fiber that broke through the faux leather armrests. Deep in thought, he exhaled sharply, the blemished mahogany in his eyes sparkling as he moved his face closer to Susan and Mia. "Well, we have two options. One: you two go out there again and see what you can find. Two: you stay here – I'll hide you – until six AM."

Susan bit her lower lip. "Do we have a third option?" she asked.

"I'm afraid not. We are out of ideas."

"Do you think there's still people alive in this damned building?" Susan looked at Mia. "Sorry...I meant this bloody building – no pun intended."

Mr. Mukh snorted from laughter. Susan smiled.

"What if Mia stays here for a while and I go down and see if there's anyone left to save – or to *take out*?"

"It's a plan," Mr. Mukh muttered.

"What about my mommy?" Mia asked with a scared, pleading voice. A sharp pang of guilt washed over Susan. She didn't make eye contact with Mia. Mr. Mukh nodded when Susan caught him staring at the little girl. "Mr. Mukh, do you know my mommy?"

The old man touched his beard and beamed at Mia. "I met your mom once or twice. Lovely girl, just like you."

"Do you think my mommy went to get help?"

Mr. Mukh glanced at Susan, who lowered her head. "I don't know, Mia. Perhaps she did. But why don't we think of good things, yes? I still have some ice cream – would you like some?"

Mia nodded sharply, and Mr. Mukh lumbered to the kitchen. Susan took Mia's hand, and a few minutes later, Mr. Mukh brought Mia a bowl of vanilla ice cream and a large, pink plastic spoon. "Eat, my dear, you need the strength."

Mia didn't have to be told twice. She slobbered up the ice cream in less than three bites, and her smiling face was smeared with vanilla ice cream. Susan wiped it off with her hands.

"Eeeew!" Mia protested.

Unexpectedly, and without warning, Susan began to tremble all over and felt the sudden urge to sleep. The room spun around like she was on some crazy Merry-Go-Round. She grabbed Mia for support but noticed that the little girl was already fast asleep. Susan looked at Mr. Mukh. "Whash hap...happening to...me?" She could barely speak.

Mr. Mukh's embracing smile turned venomous. "You won't die," he said, quite matter of fact.

Susan's ears filled with loud static. She couldn't see properly anymore. As she attempted to stand up, her legs gave out and she smashed against the couch. Sleep soon took over.

"Goodnight," Mr. Mukh whispered.

JOHANN WEITZER SCREAMED. A loud, guttural, semi-demonic shriek that filled the halls of Weitzer Technologies and his technicians cowered in fear. Seated around an oblong table

Weitzer had called a meeting with his top tech guys as something was wrong with the feed – Susan and Mia had disappeared, and after numerous attempts to locate them, the system had merely bugged out and regurgitated error codes like binary vomit.

"*What the fuck is going on?*" Weitzer slammed a fist into the table. Jacques, one of the lead technicians, attempted to calm him down. "Mr. Weitzer, the fault is not on our side. Please, I urge you to remain calm while we figure this out."

Weitzer didn't like being talked down to. He stomped towards Jacques, grabbed the man by the collar and yelled, "You *urge* me – Johann Weitzer – to *calm down*? We are losing money by the second, you dumb fucker!"

Jacques nodded, not because he agreed, but because he was terrified of the man.

Another daring technician – Weitzer didn't even know his name – ventured with a theory, "What if they're hiding somewhere?"

Weitzer turned to him. "What?"

"What if they found a space they could hide in? Somewhere no one knows about?"

"We'd have picked up their heat signals," Johann barked.

"What if – and just hear me out – what if this place *cannot* be tracked for heat signals or temp readings? What if it's just a dead zone?"

The technician had a point. Weitzer considered his options.

"Your theory could be correct. However, if we can't trace them, we can't bet on them. That means we lose money." Weitzer sat down, his face flushed with anger.

"I have an idea?" It was another technician, a blossoming brunette who wore a halter-neck and CK perfume. Weitzer was stunned by her beauty.

"Go ahead – what's your name again?"

"Eva Gorman, sir."

"Eva, tell me your idea."

She cleared her throat. "Correct me if I'm wrong, Mr. Weitzer, but we have full control over the *War Game*, do we not?"

"Define *full control*." Weitzer was visibly less irritated by the woman.

"We can remotely activate the explosives, unjam the signal blockers, and switch off the electricity...can't we?"

"Yes. So?" Weitzer furrowed his brow.

"Why don't we switch off the power, unjam the signal blockers and set a timer on the explosives? What if we bring in a twist and push the six AM deadline up a bit? Say four-thirty?"

"That makes no sense whatsoever, Eva." Weitzer was annoyed again.

"Let's smoke them out, sir. Set off an explosive or two? Shake things up a bit? They'll soon scurry out of their hiding spot." Eva grinned, her teeth unbelievably white.

"Jesus, you are clever, aren't you?" Weitzer looked at her. She adjusted her breasts slightly and blushed, unsure as to whether it was a compliment or not.

"Thank you? I guess?"

"Let's do it. Everyone! Listen up! We're going to set off explosives 110 and 111. They're on the eastern side of the building. Eva, can you check with engineering and find out whether the explosions could cause irreversible structural damage? We don't want to kill them yet, just a spook or two."

Eva nodded. "I'm on it, sir."

"Oh, and Eva?"

She stopped and looked into Weitzer 's ice-eyes.

"Sir?"

"You're now my new personal assistant."

"Uhm, what about Helena?"

"She quit. Up for it?"

Eva grinned excitedly. "Yes! I mean, yes, sir!"

CAPTAIN FERNANDO FLOREZ had never slept properly after 9/ 11. The doctors called it Post-Traumatic Stress Disorder, he called it "being fucked up".

He'd lost his brother in the attack, he'd been a firefighter. Fernando never quite processed the grief and anger he felt towards Al-Qaeda, the government, and terrorists in general. Hardly a Muslim hater, Fernando often defended the mosques and his Muslim friends in the press. That single event, however, had polarized New York. Some called him a traitor, while others labeled him a "peace negotiator".

Fernando, one of the first Hispanic immigrants to become Captain of the NYPD, never wanted hatred to cloud his judgment. Some people were evil, that couldn't be denied, but the goodness in the world equaled the horror at every turn. Therefore, instead of hating everyone and growing bitter like his father, Fernando embraced both his job and personal life to the fullest and never fully accepting the murderous intent that had taken away Fernando's brother, best friend and hero.

Fernando was also a keen observer, not just of people, but also of life in general, and had a knack of being able to pick up on those things which often remained unsaid in conversations.

After sending his best detective, Marita Merkovitz, over to the Murray building, Fernando had expected her to call with an update. This, of course had never happened, and when Fernando tried to phone her, it had immediately gone to voicemail and he'd left the detective several urgent messages.

Frustrated, Fernando got out of bed, poured himself a slice of whiskey and stared at his reflection in the kitchen window. Something was definitely amiss; Detective Merkovitz was impeccable to a fault with her punctuality.

Fernando plucked his iPhone from the wall charger in the kitchen. *No calls.*

Detective Merkovitz usually dialed through on his personal number, or she'd send an *iMessage* to alert him of something important.

But there was nothing, the only notification he'd received was an email from Kindle, asking if he was interested in the new Stephen King novel.

Fernando considered phoning Deputy Lorrence, the only other police officer, aside from Detective Merkovitz of course, whom he trusted with his life. Mind made up, he dialed Lorrence's direct line.

"Captain! What a surprise!"

"Yes, yes, spare me the insomnia lectures."

Lorrence laughed. "What can I do for you on this fine night, sir?"

"Something is bothering me, Paul." Fernando always referred to Lorrence by his first name – the man had practically lived with Fernando and his wife for two years. Divorce. Two kids. The usual.

"Bothering you? What's up, Fernando?" Paul Lorrence switched over to informality quicker than Fernando could blink.

"I don't know... I sent Merkovitz out to the Murray Building to check on Officer Lindsey Moss. Have you heard anything?"

A long pause. Fernando shifted his weight. What was Paul hiding from him?

"Okay, so, this is weird –" Paul coughed.

"What's weird, Paul?" Fernando knew the guy better than his own son. And he definitely knew when Paul was hiding something.

"I received a call about an hour ago. A woman from Switzerland. Helena something, I think?" Paul cleared his throat – an obvious sign that he was feeling uncomfortable. "She wanted to speak to you, Fernando. But I told her that you weren't in. She was quite demanding and, I must admit, somewhat rude. Anyways, long story short, she told me that she *knew for a fact* that Detective Merkovitz and Officer Moss were *dead*. I didn't believe her, so she sent me to a website, right? Gave me her password and everything. Then the line went dead."

Fernando poured another glass of whiskey. "Go ahead, Paul."

"Then her boss phoned – guess who her boss is?"

"Jesus?"

"No, Johann Weitzer!"

Fernando gasped. "*The* Johann Weitzer? The rich Swiss guy?"

"You've got it."

"Why on earth did he phone you, Paul? Surely he has personal assistants or robots or some shit to do that for him?"

"He told me that the Dutch girl was an ex-employee of his and – get this – that she suffered from severe schizophrenia."

Fernando's annoyance with Paul's lackadaisical attitude reached a fever pitch.

"Paul, you know you're like a son to me, yeah?"

"Yes?"

"So, please don't get offended when I ask you, why *the fuck* didn't you investigate the matter further?" Fernando's voice rumbled through the house.

"I-I-I didn't think about it any further, you know? We get so many crank calls –"

Fernando cut him off, "Check when Officer Moss last radioed in."

Paul put Fernando on hold. Several seconds passed as Fernando's Latin blood boiled. Paul's voice came back on the line – it was timid and withered.

"Eight PM. She investigated a random noise complaint."

"And no one in the entire NYPD thought about contacting her?" Fernando was livid. "Jesus H. Christ, Paul! I'm coming down there right now. Hang up the phone, and try to locate Moss and Merkovitz."

Paul stammered, "B-b-but..."

"Deputy Lorrence, *do your fucking job!*" Fernando barked and tossed the iPhone into the living room. It hit the couch and tumbled to the carpeted floor. As Fernando rushed to the bedroom to get dressed – *civilian is fine* – he bumped into his wife, Carmen. She stood at the foot of the stairs, arms crossed, nose upturned, nostrils flaring. "What in all that is holy is going on at this time of the night?"

Fernando replied meekly, "Carmen, baby, there's some trouble at the station. I gotta go."

"It's three-thirty in the goddamned morning! Can't it wait?"

"No, honey. You know the job..."

She calmed a little and hugged him. "I'll make sandwiches."

Fernando kissed his wife on the cheek and rushed up the stairs to get dressed. All hell was breaking loose in Fernando's mind, and for the first time in his long, illustrious career, he had a feeling that this was the end of the road.

CHAPTER FOUR
4:00AM

Magai had searched every single room in the entire building. Not one living soul. Dead bodies, yes, plenty of those, with their claw-like hands and spilled intestines.

He paced around the fifth floor; There had to be something he'd missed. The game definitely wasn't over, so where were the survivors? What if Magai had already won, but there was no one around to tell him? No, no, Magai dispelled those negative thoughts. He'd waited this long – he wasn't going to go gently into that long goodnight; patience was Magai's most promising virtue, along with a healthy dose of revenge-lust.

Magai looked in every corner, glanced at every shadow, and listened to every sound – searching for anything to indicate that he wasn't as alone as he thought he was.

Click.

The sound came from the stairwell. Magai held his sword and hurried, knees bent, to locate its origin. As he reached the end of the hallway, Magai noticed something peculiar. There, in a dark corner of the fifth floor, was a small, brass latch. Curious, Magai pulled on it and found himself at the foot of a wooden staircase.

Darkness whirled around him, a blank, cheap smell wafted from above. Magai ascended the staircase like a cat, treading carefully, silently.

A dim, bronze light flickered at the very end of the hallway. Magai hadn't registered just how short the staircase actually was – just seven steps. Surprised by his unexpected discovery, Magai headed inside without hesitation, curious, anxious and terrified all at once.

His breathing slowed down.

Three steps, four steps, five steps, and then Magai found himself at the entrance to what appeared to be a hidden attic apartment. He couldn't believe it. This was it! This was the proverbial Road to Enlightenment.

Magai didn't see Mr. Mukh in the darkness, nor did he notice Mia and Susan's sleeping bodies on the couch; the light had switched off just as Magai came up the stairs.

"Magai Nyasaka. In the flesh." A shadowed man rose to his feet and quickly closed the gap between them. *Old, white scraggly beard, definitely of Islamic origin* – the man stuck out a hand. Magai, unable to discern the level of danger he was in, shook the man's hand.

"My name is Mr. Mukh. Of course, I know who you are, Magai, so no need for formal introductions."

Magai was surprised that this odd man knew who he was. "How do you know my name?" he asked.

"I know *everything*. I know about Bethany Anderson, Marita Merkovitz, and Samuel Murray losing all of your money. I also know that you came here for revenge, isn't that so, Magai?" Mr. Mukh spoke softly, in delicate tones.

"You cannot know these things, unless you were one of Samuel Murray's *whores*!" Magai flicked his sword through the air.

Mr. Mukh didn't even flinch. "Lower your sword."

"Or what?" Magai was tempted to slice off the man's head right then and there and make a run for the entrance, the bizarre nature of the meeting scared him so much.

"Or I do what I am supposed to do." Mr. Mukh switched on the light. Magai took a step back when he saw Susan and Mia on the couch. "Who are they?" he demanded.

"They are none of your concern."

"Oh! So *this* is how you do it? You drug people and then walk out when the game ends. Easy way to earn $100 million! No blood on your dirty Muslim hands!"

A bright flash of startling white light erupted from Mr. Mukh's hip and a searing shard of pain shoved Magai against the wall.

His leg felt wet and numb, Magai touched the dampness that pooled near his ankle – hot, sticky blood, he'd been shot in the leg.

Years of pent up rage filled Magai, ignoring the pain that shot through his wounded leg, hee swiped his sword through the air, arcing it down towards Mr. Mukh's chest. Mr. Mukh moved away just in time, and stood opposite Magai and smiled at the man like a giddy child.

"Don't worry, Magai, I'm not going to kill you. I just want to tell you a story."

"A story? You're as good as dead, you Muslim trash!"

Another bright flash. Magai's hand splintered. Blood spurted from the ragged wound. He dropped the sword, two fingers missing from his right hand, three of the knuckles ripped to shreds.

"You *fucking...*" Magai collapsed, the shock too much for his aging body to handle.

Mr. Mukh grabbed Magai by the feet and dragged him into the living room. The man was alive, but Mr. Mukh knew he'd be unconscious long enough for his final plan to take effect.

THE PHONE RANG OUT on Weitzer's desk. He picked up the receiver and barked, "What is it?" Only a select few employees had the direct line to his office, and they usually used it to complain about something or other.

The person on the other end of the line was in the throes of a coughing fit. Frustrated, Weitzer pinched the bridge of his nose. *Jesus,* he thought.

"I do apologize for that." The man on the other end of the line wasn't an employee. Weitzer froze – no one, *no one*, except for the chosen few had his direct number.

"May I ask to whom I am speaking?" Weitzer managed to keep his annoyance at bay.

"Little Johann Weitzer – just look at you now, all loud and proud, like some faggot pride parade!"

What. The. Fuck.

"*Excuse me*? Who the fuck is this?"

"Till voices wake us and we drown. It's from *The Love song of J Alfred Prufrock* by T.S. Eliot. You know it?"

The man was distinctly American, his accent loaded with a New York lilt.

"Listen, I don't know who you are or how you got this number, but I don't have time for riddles, so goodbye –"

"Wait," the man demanded.

"For what? I'm disconnecting this call now."

"Do it and you'll be bankrupt before close of business tomorrow. You and all of your staff will also be arrested."

Weitzer felt unbridled hysteria and anger boiling up inside of him. "Are you threatening me? You *old* fuck!"

"No, Johann, I am *advising* you." The man coughed again. Weitzer imagined bloody phlegm sputtering from the old man's mouth. He shivered.

"So, what's your angle? Huh? This is not the first time I've been threatened by crazy people. *Scheisse.*"

"My name is Captain Fernando Florez, and this is not your *War Game*."

Weitzer burst into slightly insane laughter.

"Seriously? What's next? You're the ghost from Christmas past? Listen, old man –"

"You're currently streaming the *War Game* to what? Three billion people? You were attacked by a pit bull when you were seven. You still have a scar on your left index finger. Your father, also Johann, went to the property where the attack took place and shot the dog –point blank. You were there and you still hear the sound that dying pit bull made when you close your eyes at night. Oh, and Helena Erasmus? Beautiful execution."

Weitzer dropped the receiver and vomited over his desk. Never before, not even when the pit bull attacked him, had he experienced such terror. To him, the authorities were an embodiment of Satan himself, and if they found out that he owned the rights to what amounted to a global snuff film, Weitzer Technologies would be finished.

A knock on the door startled Weitzer. "Come!" he croaked.

Eva Gorman, dressed in a tight-fitting, red dress, entered, her face as white as a Swiss winter. "Sir, we have a problem."

Weitzer rested his head between his hands. "What is it now?" he asked, defeated.

"Someone took it upon himself to decide the outcome of the *War Game*."

"*What?*" Weitzer asked, a string of yellow vomit dribbling from his chin.

"We have identified him as one Ahmed Mukh. Born in India, he left for the States when he was five – sir, you have to see this to believe it." Eva grabbed the remote on Weitzer's desk and switched on the TV.

Magai Nyasaka, Mia Corletti and Susan Sussman were tied to chair in what looked like a basement apartment. Ahmed Mukh stood before them with a remote in his hands.

"Where did he get that fucking remote? Eva?"

"Sir, we rewound the videos – he took it from Benjamin Sussman's pocket. That remote, when activated, will end the game and bring down the building."

Weitzer leapt from his seat. "Tell tech to halt the detonations; this is better than I ever imagined it could be."

"Already done, sir. May I ask what happened in here?" Eva's blade blue eyes stared at the congealing pool of vomit on Weitzer's desk.

"We have a another problem, Eva. I just got off the phone with a Captain Fernando Florez, NYPD. He knows. The authorities *know*."

Eva staggered back, her face slack. "That cannot be!" she was now the hysterical one.

"They're most probably already on their way, and Interpol will be here before tomorrow. Destroy everything."

"Sir, we can't -"

"Double the bets, pay 10% severance and – wait, what is the total amount currently?"

Eva checked her phone.

"Seven billion dollars in bets, sir."

"Who's in the lead?"

"It switches between Susan Sussman and Mia Corletti every minute, sir."

"Destroy the evidence – *now, Eva!*"

CAPTAIN FLOREZ SAT with the phone receiver cradled in his hand. Florez's Ccellphone rang out, *Marita Merkovitz* flasheing up on the screen. Fernando exhaled loudly and thumbed the answer button.

"Marita! Where are you?"

"This isn't Marita Merkovitz, Captain."

"Who is this?" Florez's veins bulged in his neck.

"My name is Ahmed Mukh, you may call me *Mr.* Mukh." The voice was infuriatingly calm and steady.

"We're sending a SWAT team to that god forsaken building right now, and I swear to God, *Ahmed Mukh*, if any of this is your doing, you'll –"

"This is *not* my doing, sir. I am merely the one who ends it."

"Ends what?" Florez screamed.

Mr. Mukh told him about the *War Game* and Samuel Murray's decade-long involvement. What he said next sent hysterical chills down Fernando's spine.

"...the building is wired with explosives. If you, or any of your men attempt to breach the building, it *will* blow up. The final three *will* die. Do things my way and I am able to control things and have one of them survive."

Captain Florez shifted in his seat.

"You cannot do this, Ahmed. You are going to kill innocent people. I already know about the three billion people watching..."

"Then you know that I have to see this through."

"Are you an employee of Samuel Murray?"

Mr. Mukh cleared his throat and spoke in a hushed tone, "Quite the opposite, in fact. I am here to protect the legacy of Gregor Karpov, a Russian national who gave his life to Samuel Murray."

"Ahmed –"

"Please, Captain Florez, call me Mr. Mukh. I hate my name."

"Mr. Mukh, it is. I shall be sending the entire NYPD, plus the FBI to the Murray building. You will *not* get away with this!"

The line went dead.

Fernando Florez, the man who thought he knew everything, was at an impasse. He had no option but to send every person he had, but what if their arrival sent Mukh over the edge?

"Captain? You have to see this." A female officer, Samantha Killborne, had a laptop open in her hands. She set it down in front of Florez. At first, he didn't recognize the scene – it looked like a feed from a poor man's excuse for a CCTV camera. He tried to focus his sleep-deprived mind on the scene playing out on the screen.

There, in the poor light of a basement apartment stood Mr. Ahmed Mukh. He had three people tied chairs, and there were numbers and names superimposed at the bottom of the screen:

MIA CORLETTI - $3.1 BILLION
SUSAN SUSSMAN - $3 BILLION
MAGAI NYASAKA - $1 BILLION

"Can we get audio on that?" Florez asked. Killbourne pressed a couple of buttons. Static, followed by clear audio spilled out of the laptop speakers.

THE FINALE:
PRISONERS OF WAR PLAY RUSSIAN ROULETTE

4:45AM

"**W**ho am I? What is my purpose? If I were a character in a novel, I'd be cast as the neutral protagonist, the final stick of dynamite needed for that big explosion at the end. Well, ladies and gentle*man*, I am about to share with you the very purpose behind my existence in this whole charade." Mr. Mukh's voice stirred Susan awake, his words sticking in her brain. Her eyes flickered open.

Mia and an old Japanese man sat on either sides of her. As Susan struggled out of her drugged slumber, she began to notice her surroundings, the old, couch, the television playing static, the fluorescent bathroom light, and above all that the strange, deadly smell that lingered near her nostrils.

"Ah, Susan!" Mr. Mukh clasped his hands together. "Welcome! This was my old friend, Gregor Karpov's apartment. You might know it?"

Susan couldn't move, her body was bound to a metal chair by stiff leather straps. Terror raged through her, her every nerve ending tingling.

Mia looked across at Susan. Her own mouth was covered by duct tape. The Japanese man was in the same situation as them, bound to a metal chair, mouth sealed with the silver tape.

"Okay, now that everyone is present and accounted for, let's begin, shall we?"

Susan moaned out loud and struggled to pull free from the restraints that held her tight.

"Susan, not you, Mia, nor Magai will be able to break free. So calm down, please?" Mr. Mukh cleared his throat. "Gregor Karpov lived here for almost his entire life. He gave me everything – a place to call home, friendship, money and family. I helped him smuggle his daughter and wife into the country. I hid them in the attic for several years, but sadly, Gregor became antsy.

In 1997, a couple of weeks before the Merkovitz massacre, Gregor and I agreed that his wife and daughter should move to his basement apartment. However, one Benjamin Sussman – who worked for Samuel Murray – shot and killed Gregor's wife and daughter."

Mr. Mukh took a sip of tea.

"After his grief subsided, Gregor and I worked tirelessly to solve Samuel Murray's cryptic message about his *War Game*. To cut a long story short – we really do have to go soon – I became obsessed with it; so obsessed in fact, that I eventually knew more about the *War Game* than Samuel Murray did.

I took it upon myself to investigate everything; the building's tumultuous history, Samuel Murray's questionable business dealings, the Bethany Anderson abduction – she looked the spitting image of Marita Merkovitz, so good for you, Magai – and the role we'd all have to play one day. Protagonists and antagonists, saints and sinners, killers and lovers – all of us would come together to untie the final knot that was Samuel Murray's ingenious *War Game*."

Mr. Mukh took a seat on Gregor's couch. He eyed the final three players with horrific intensity.

"So, here comes the final part. The police are on their way – I already phoned them. However, we cannot allow them to interfere. *I* cannot allow them to interfere. While you were all running around like headless chickens, more than three billion people tuned in to the web stream to watch the *War Game* unfold, and they placed their wagers on all three of you."

Mia cried. Susan looked at her and tried to assuage the little girl's fears.

"This here is a remote. The *real* remote. See the red button?" He showed it to each one of the three in turn. "That sets off the explosives. Boom!

The rules of the game state that only one person can survive, and since we can't waste time having you three battling it out, I took the initiative to declare one of you the winner based on the amount of bets were placed on you. At exactly 4:59AM, one of you will be freed from your restraints; you will have exactly sixty seconds to get out of the building – the front entrance is now unlocked. Second and third place, well...you *will* perish alongside me. We'll all die together. So you see, I'm not a contestant – I'm the neutral protagonist."

Susan closed her eyes and prayed. Mia stared at Mr. Mukh like he was some kind of big, scary monster. And Magai, well, Magai sobbed.

Mr. Mukh ripped the duct tape from their mouths. "Don't scream. Your final words will be remembered forever." Mr. Mukh was most calm, which was unsettling, given the circumstances.

Magai spoke first. "You cannot do this! It is against the rules! We *have* to fight it out!" Annoyed, Mr. Mukh silenced Magai with more duct tape.

Susan knew she had to say something, something important, historic, and something which might just sway the final bets in Mia's favor. "Please, to all of you watching this, please don't let this little girl die. I ask you all to have mercy. *Please*!" Duct tape covered Susan's mouth once again.

Mia remained silent. She looked like someone who'd survived some horrible genocide, and Mr. Mukh didn't use the duct tape on Mia, because he knew the child was long gone.

Mr. Mukh reached into his pocket and pulled out an iPhone. He'd unjammed the signals earlier, in order to access the betting tallies. He smiled, sighed and gave each of the final three a small hug.

"God be with you all. I have the results. We have two minutes before the only survivor is freed from his –

or her – restraints. $100 million will be given to you by someone who used to work for Samuel Murray and you can be on your way.

And – it's time. Remember to run as fast as you can. Get far away from the building. Do what you have to do to escape the blast zone.

Ten seconds remaining – goodnight, and good luck, as Samuel liked to say."

9

8

7

6

5

4

3

2

1

THE EXPLOSION WASN'T as bad as she thought it would be. The blast zone was contained, and the building came down within moments. None of the surrounding buildings suffered any structural damage. It was as if the Murray building had just decided enough was enough and crumple in on itself.

She did as Mr. Mukh instructed – she ran so fast that her heart almost ripped itself out of her chest, and her feet bled.

When the police came, they swarmed through the gutted remains of what was once the most infamous project in New York history. And she looked on as the day broke across the horizon. Someone clad in black – a woman, possibly it was impossible to tell for sure – placed a briefcase at her feet.

The contents were what she expected it to be: $100 million in cold, hard-won cash.

EPILOGUE

After his humiliating arrest by Interpol, Johann Weitzer was found guilty of fraud, embezzlement, and murder. He received a whole life sentence and would never taste freedom again.

Weitzer Technologies closed down – the employees were all arrested and sentenced according to their *War Game* wagers for being complicit. The truth about Maddy Murray captivated the world's attention for several months, but as with all news stories, Maddy Murray died quietly as a footnote on a conspiracy blog. Bethany Anderson, the *real* Maddy, was given a headstone in a lonely cemetery; her parents finally able to grieve their missing daughter's death.

Captain Fernando Florez and Deputy Paul Lorrence went their separate ways. Lorrence was suspended from the force after a disciplinary committee found him guilty of gross negligence. Although a criminal case was opened against him, Captain Florez begged the District Attorney for leniency, and his old friend was let go with little more than a slap on the wrist.

Captain Florez never saw Deputy Paul Lorrence again.

War Game became one of the most reported stories of its time. Thousands of opinionated journalists and armchair critics dissected the story until it was nothing more than a white bone buried in the back gardens of gossipmongers. Footage eventually leaked out, and the whole got to watch the *War Game* as bootleg DVDs and torrent sites provided cheap access to the most horrific snuff film ever created.

She who survived the horrors of that night placed the money in a trust, never to be touched unless it meant gaining revenge on those who had wronged her. It took her five years to sleep properly again, and another two years before she could integrate back into society. Everyone knew her name, but the winner of the *War Game* refused to acknowledge her own identity; she went entirely off the grid shortly after the release of the Hollywood blockbuster, *War Game: A Documentary*.

The survivor, the winner, the one who beat the most terrifying odds became an ephemeral, anonymous entity, a ghost of sorts. She held on to the only truths she could understand: vengeance, retribution and finally, if time allowed, absolution.

TO BE CONTINUED...

Don't miss out!

Visit the website below and you can sign up to receive emails whenever Renier Palland publishes a new book. There's no charge and no obligation.

https://books2read.com/r/B-A-BOUR-IUJWB

BOOKS 2 READ

Connecting independent readers to independent writers.

About the Author

Renier Palland was born in South Africa, but received American citizenship through his PhD degrees in the fields of Sociology, Film and Epidemiology, among others. (His agent advised against listing all of his academic achievements, "because hubris doesn't sell well")

Well into his early-30's, Renier had already accomplished an abundance of daring literary feats, most notably War Game's spin-off being optioned for an Amazon Prime mini-series, his debut poetry book garnering critical acclaim, and the first book of the War Game trilogy being lauded by critics as "the book of year." This, along with numerous other writing accolades, gave him the courage to always challenge the status quo through his writings.

Renier enjoys waxing lyrical about the human condition, often referring to life as "a mess of beautiful contradictions".

He is an activist, a fighter for justice and equality, and a proud member of several human rights organizations.

Alleviate the suffering of all living beings, even at the expense of one's own suffering.